CM

St. Helens Libraries

Please return / renew this item by the last date shown.
Books may also be renewed by phone and Internet.

Telephone – (01744) 676954 or 677822
Email – centrallibrary@sthelens.gov.uk
Online – http://eps.sthelens.gov.uk/rooms

E22 May 23

- 1 FEB 2019

2 2 FEB 2019

1 6 AUG 2019

DEC 23

✔ KU-545-104

ST.HELENS COMMUNITY LIBRARY

3 8055 01314 1775

Carol Marinelli recently filled in a form asking for her job title. Thrilled to be able to put down her answer, she put 'writer'. Then it asked what Carol did for relaxation and she put down the truth—'writing'. The third question asked for her hobbies. Well, not wanting to look obsessed, she crossed her fingers and answered 'swimming'— but, given that the chlorine in the pool does terrible things to her highlights, I'm sure you can guess the real answer!

Also by Carol Marinelli

Seduced by the Sheikh Surgeon
Playboy on Her Christmas List
Their Secret Royal Baby
Their One Night Baby
Sicilian's Baby of Shame
Claiming His Hidden Heir

Ruthless Royal Sheikhs miniseries

Captive for the Sheikh's Pleasure
Christmas Bride for the Sheikh

Discover more at millsandboon.co.uk.

THE MIDWIFE'S ONE-NIGHT FLING

CAROL MARINELLI

ST. HELENS
COMMUNITY
LIBRARIES

ACC. No.

CLASS No.

MILLS & BOON

All rights reserved including the right of reproduction in whole or in part in any form. This edition is published by arrangement with Harlequin Books S.A.

This is a work of fiction. Names, characters, places, locations and incidents are purely fictional and bear no relationship to any real life individuals, living or dead, or to any actual places, business establishments, locations, events or incidents. Any resemblance is entirely coincidental.

This book is sold subject to the condition that it shall not, by way of trade or otherwise, be lent, resold, hired out or otherwise circulated without the prior consent of the publisher in any form of binding or cover other than that in which it is published and without a similar condition including this condition being imposed on the subsequent purchaser.

® and TM are trademarks owned and used by the trademark owner and/or its licensee. Trademarks marked with ® are registered with the United Kingdom Patent Office and/or the Office for Harmonisation in the Internal Market and in other countries.

First published in Great Britain 2018
by Mills & Boon, an imprint of HarperCollins*Publishers*
1 London Bridge Street, London, SE1 9GF

Large Print edition 2018

© 2018 Carol Marinelli

ISBN: 978-0-263-07313-3

MIX
Paper from
responsible sources
FSC™ C007454

This book is produced from independently certified FSC™ paper to ensure responsible forest management. For more information visit www.harpercollins.co.uk/green.

Printed and bound in Great Britain
by CPI Group (UK) Ltd, Croydon, CR0 4YY

Dear Lucinda
Love you more xxxx

PROLOGUE

'YOU MUST BE getting excited about the big move to London?'

It was a question Freya Ross had heard many times in recent weeks, and although the knot in her stomach tightened at the thought of what lay ahead she smiled.

'I'm very much looking forward to it.'

As a midwife at the birthing centre attached to Cromayr Bay Hospital, Freya was examining Mrs Roberts while her three little boys ran amok in the rather small cubicle. Most patients preferred to be called by their first name, but not Mrs Roberts.

'Jamie!' Mrs Roberts scolded as her boisterous three-year-old climbed on a chair.

Freya was more than used to working with toddlers underfoot, and she was also very used to holding in her thoughts.

She had told no one of her misgivings about

moving to London. Not her parents, nor her best friend, nor her colleagues. Certainly she would not burden a patient with her worries.

No one could possibly guess that now her leaving date was almost here Freya was dreading making the move from the small Scottish town of Cromayr Bay to London.

The news of her leaving had come as a complete surprise to everyone. No one had known she'd gone to London for an interview. This was no mean feat in Cromayr Bay! Even swapping her off-duty days had been complicated—Freya hadn't been able to lie and say that she was visiting the dentist, given that the dentist was the husband of Betty, her senior midwife. And, had she called in sick—well someone would either have mentioned that her car had been seen at Cromayr Bay station, or they'd have dropped in to check that she was okay.

In the end Freya had said that she was catching up with a friend with whom she had trained.

'Oh? Who?' Betty had asked…

Feeling as if her nose must surely be an inch longer after such a complex lie, Freya had taken the train to Edinburgh's Waverley Station and from there had travelled down to London to the Primary, a large, modern hospital.

Freya's general nursing training had taken place in Cowdenbeath, and she had done some placements in Edinburgh during her midwifery training, so she wasn't unfamiliar with busy hospitals. The Primary was incredibly large, though, and the interview had been very thorough.

Her training had been excellent, and Freya had kept her skills up to date with regular shifts in the main Cromayr Bay hospital, which the birthing centre was attached to.

She had been offered a six-month contract by the London hospital, commencing in the middle of July, and Freya was starting to get nervous.

Not that she showed it.

Instead of revealing her feelings now, she made small talk with Mrs Roberts as she palpated the baby. 'We've got my leaving do tonight, over at the Tavern,' Freya said. 'You're actually the last patient that I'll see before I go.'

'I'm sorry that you shan't be here for the birth.'

'I am too, Mrs Roberts,' Freya agreed. 'Although I know you are going to do just fine.'

'I expect Alison is feeling the same as I do about your leaving?'

Freya's hands paused mid-examination. Alison had made it clear that she didn't want the news about her pregnancy getting out just yet.

'We're best friends.' Freya decided to give a non-committal answer, just in case she had misinterpreted the question. 'So, yes, she was a bit upset when I told her that I was moving—but I'll be coming home regularly.'

'I meant about the baby,' Mrs Roberts said. 'It's okay, I'm not asking you to break any confidences. I just heard the other day that she's expecting again. It's lovely news.'

'It is,' Freya agreed, though inwardly she sighed for her friend at the fact that the news had got out. Very few people knew. And, even though Alison was past her first trimester, she had wanted to keep it to herself for a while yet.

But nothing stayed a secret for very long here.

'I just hope…' Mrs Roberts voice trailed off.

'Well,' she said. 'I hope that things go better for her this time.'

Freya gave a small nod, but refused to be drawn into a discussion about the loss of Andrew.

Last year had been a hard one.

Following an uneventful pregnancy, Alison had arrived at the birthing centre in active labour. But while checking the foetal heart-rate Freya had realised something was terribly wrong.

Alison had been transferred to the attached hospital and a crash Caesarean had been performed. The little boy had been resuscitated and then transferred to Edinburgh, where there had been a NICU cot available.

He'd been beautiful and utterly perfect. A chunky baby, with long, dark lashes, big cheeks and pudgy hands. But the lack of oxygen from cord compression and subsequent meconium aspiration had left him severely brain damaged.

Despite best efforts Andrew had died two days later, leaving Alison, her husband Callum and their families shattered.

Freya had been his godmother and proxy aunt, and she still woke regularly from nightmares, with the ominous sound of the CTG bleeping seeming to fill her bedroom. It felt as if her chest was being crushed whenever she recalled the devastation on Alison's face when it had become clear that things were going terribly wrong.

'*Freya?*' Alison had pleaded.

The fear in Alison's voice was something that Freya would never be able to erase from her memory.

Alison had never blamed Freya. In fact she had drawn on her friend, and Freya had stayed strong for Alison even through a serious relationship break-up.

And now, not by a flicker did she reveal her own heartache as she focussed on her patient and the little life beneath her hands.

'Everything's looking grand,' Freya said as she felt the baby's position. 'The head is down and baby is a good size.'

'Aye.'

For Freya, the real beauty of working at Cromayr Bay was the chance to really get to know her patients and their families, and now, after being more than willing to chat about Alison's pregnancy, Mrs Roberts's short response when discussing her own, concerned Freya.

It wasn't just that, though. Over the months Freya had been trying to gauge Mrs Roberts's feelings.

This pregnancy had come close after the birth of twins, but Mrs Roberts insisted it was all part of the plan as she wanted her children to be near each other in age.

Freya was quite certain that Mrs Roberts was struggling, but she was a very proud and private woman. Earlier, though, she'd seemed more talkative, and Freya wondered if she actually wanted to speak to her.

Jamie, the eldest, was getting restless, and the twins were going through their mother's handbag. Freya was in no doubt that Mrs Roberts would want to dash off as soon as her appointment was done.

As she went to the desk to write up her findings Mrs Roberts dressed and then came over and took a seat.

'Jamie!' She scolded her son, who had pulled over a jar of cotton balls. 'I'm so sorry, Freya.'

'It's not a problem. I shouldn't have left them at a three-year-old's level.' As Mrs Roberts went to retrieve them Freya stopped her. 'He might as well play with them,' she said—not just because the cotton balls would now have to be discarded, but also because it might keep Jamie amused for a few minutes.

'He's into everything,' Mrs Roberts explained. 'I need eyes in the back of my head.'

'You're certainly going to be busy when the new baby comes,' Freya agreed. 'Is there anyone who might be able to help once the baby is here?

'Och, I'll not be bothering others. I just have to get on with things.' Mrs Roberts straightened herself in the chair.

Freya felt for her. She too was very private.

With two younger brothers, Freya had always been 'the sensible one'. Her mother, Jean, had relied on her to look out for the boys and soothe their hurts rather than her own.

As Freya wrote up her notes she thought how she came across to her patient. Her long dark curls were pulled back into a ponytail and she knew that her green eyes could sometimes come across as guarded rather than shy. She was a quiet person, and that generally suited her patients just fine.

However, like Mrs Roberts, Freya could appear a touch aloof at times—abrupt, even—although not, she hoped, with her patients. And, while she tended not to chat too much about herself, that wasn't an issue in Cromayr Bay, where everyone knew everyone else's business anyway.

But Freya wanted to reach her patient and to be sure that she was coping, so she decided to open up a little to Mrs Roberts in the hope that the woman would reciprocate.

'Actually,' Freya said, 'although I'm telling everyone that I'm excited about moving to London, I'm really quite nervous. It's a big hospital and I shan't know anyone.'

'You'll be fine...' Mrs Roberts started, and then paused as Freya gently spoke on.

'I expect everyone is asking if you're excited now that the baby will soon be here?'

Mrs Roberts nodded. *"Not long now!"'* She mimicked the regular phrases being thrown daily her way. *"You'll be hoping for a girl after three boys."*

'Are you?' Freya asked. She knew the sex of the baby.

'Of course not. I didn't get pregnant to try for a girl. In fact, I didn't…' It was the closest Mrs Roberts had come to admitting the pregnancy had been an accident, but she quickly rallied. 'Healthy will suit me just fine.'

'Of course,' Freya agreed, and Mrs Roberts changed the subject.

'So you're nervous about leaving?'

'Terrified,' Freya now admitted. 'And I'm wondering how I'm going to fit in.'

'You'll fit in just fine.'

'I hope so,' Freya replied. 'But I'm starting to think I've made a mistake.'

'Well, I know *that* feeling.'

Freya watched as Mrs Roberts closed her eyes and finally admitted the truth. 'It's not that I don't want it—well, I'm sure I will once the baby's here. I just honestly don't know how I'm going to cope. The twins are into everything and Jamie runs wild. Davey's no help. Och, he tries—but he's out the door for work at seven, then not back until six and wanting his supper. I'm trying to freeze a few meals for when the baby comes…'

'That's good.'

'It'll take more than a few frozen dinners to see us through, though.'

Freya saw the flash of tears in Mrs Roberts's eyes and then watched as she buried her face in her hands and started to weep.

'Mam!' Jamie toddled over and pulled at her skirt. 'Mam!'

'Mummy's just a little tired,' Freya said as she gave Mrs Roberts some tissues.

When his inquisitive eyes fell on her stethoscope, Freya took it from her neck and played with it on him, to give Mrs Roberts time to cry by herself.

'Do you want to have a play with it now?'

Delighted with his new toy, Jamie wandered off.

'I'm sorry, Freya.' Mrs Roberts sniffed into the tissue that Freya had pressed into her hand. 'How on earth am I going to manage with another one? I don't get a moment to myself as it is.'

'Have you thought about asking your sister to

come and stay with you for a wee while once the baby arrives?' Freya knew that the two women were close.

'I have,' Mrs Roberts nodded, 'but it's a huge imposition.'

'Did she say that?'

'No, no—she offered to come. But I think it's asking too much from her.'

'You'll need help at the start, Mrs Roberts. It's better to take it than to do too much and find yourself overwhelmed and exhausted. If you talk about it with her now she can start to make plans.'

And making plans was what Freya and Mrs Roberts did next.

Her sister Norma would come, and also there was a small crèche that Mrs Roberts occasionally used.

'I might see if they can go there—just one afternoon a week, maybe two—so I can have some time with the new baby.'

'I think that's a wonderful idea,' Freya said. 'Did you know, once I've moved, I've got Mrs Hunt coming in to service my cottage between tenants?'

'I dinnae need a cleaner.'

'Well, I'm only mentioning it in case you might. She's very thorough and her prices are reasonable.'

The appointment went well over time, but it was worth every minute because Mrs Roberts was actually smiling as she retrieved the contents of her bag from the floor.

'You wee monkeys,' she said to the twins. 'Jamie, give Freya back her stethoscope.'

Before the cubicle door was opened Freya had a final word. 'If you're ever feeling overwhelmed when the baby is here—'

Mrs Roberts broke in. 'Then I'll speak to Betty. I honestly will. I feel so much better for talking with you.'

Mrs Roberts rounded up her three sons and Freya saw them to the desk. There she pulled up the appointments on the computer screen and made one for the next Thursday.

'Thanks so much, Freya.'

'You're welcome, Mrs Roberts.'

'Leah, please.'

Freya smiled, for it was high praise indeed to be invited to call Mrs Roberts by her first name.

'I wish you all the very best in London.'

'Thank you.'

Once Mrs Roberts had left Betty came over, and Freya explained a little of what had happened.

'It would have taken a lot for her to admit she's struggling,' Betty agreed. 'Well done, Freya. And don't worry—I'll be keeping a very close eye on her.'

Freya took in Betty's knowing eyes and kind face and knew Mrs Roberts was in the very best of hands. Betty had been a midwife here for nearly forty years. She had, in fact, delivered Freya herself. Right now, though, she was just trying to get the clinic closed somewhat on time.

'I'll shut down the computers and you go and tidy up the cubicles,' Betty said. 'You're going to be late for your own leaving party.'

Goodness, Freya thought when she saw the chaos of the cubicle. It looked as if it had been snowing!

Yet not for a second did she regret that the check-up had spilled more than an hour over time.

Freya tidied up and as she came out saw the waiting room was in semi-darkness.

'Everything's done,' Betty said. 'I'll lock up.'

And then it was finally here—the end of her time at the Cromayr Bay birthing centre.

Freya looked around the waiting room and beyond the desk, thinking of the two birthing suites behind. Then she walked out through the familiar room and into the office to collect her coat before a dash home to get changed for her leaving do.

She hoped her ex wouldn't show up.

Alison would be there. She had cried when Freya had told her that she was moving to London,

'I'll be back all the time,' Freya had reassured her.

'It won't be the same.'

No, it wouldn't be. But then, things hadn't been the same between them since Andrew had died.

Freya had always been private. The only person she really opened up to was Alison—but of course the loss was Alison's, so Freya had tried to remain stoic and strong for her friend, not burdening her with her own grief.

She said goodbye to Betty, who promised she would join them all at the Tavern shortly, and then drove the short distance home in her little purple car.

It was July. The holidaymakers were back and the town was busy.

She parked outside her tiny fisherman's cottage which, although a bit of a renovator's nightmare, was certainly a home.

Each of the houses along the foreshore was a different colour, and Freya's little cottage was a duck-egg-blue with a dark wooden door. Opening it, she stepped into the surprisingly large lounge with its open fireplace, seeing on the mantelpiece her favourite pictures and little mementoes.

Freya headed into the tiny alcove kitchen. It needed a complete overhaul, but everything worked—and anyway, Freya wasn't much of a cook. In pride of place was a coffee machine that Freya was having to leave behind in the move, as there really wasn't that much room in her father's car.

It would be nice for the tenants, Freya thought as she made a very quick coffee.

Freya had the house rented out over the summer, but in October it was going on the market to be sold.

In the cellar she had boxed up some of her belongings. The tiny spare bedroom looked a little bare, but it was ready for its new occupant with a pretty wrought-iron bed and a small chest of drawers.

Freya headed into the main bedroom to change out of her uniform and get ready for her leaving do, but for a moment she paused.

The unobstructed view of The Firth had sold the place to her on sight. Often at night she simply lay there in bed, looking out, and she had watched the new Queensferry crossing being built. It was a spectacular cable-stayed bridge, and Freya had watched the huge structure unfold from either side until finally the two sides had met.

It was her favourite view on earth, and as she gazed out to it Freya asked herself again what the hell she was doing leaving. Here, she had a job she loved and friends she had grown up with as well as her family, to whom she was very close.

Yet, the very things she loved about Cromayr

Bay, were the very reasons she felt she had to leave.

The loss of Alison's baby had hit everyone.

After it had happened Freya had often walked into a shop or a café, and on too many occasions the conversation would suddenly stop.

Everyone knew everyone's business—which wasn't always a good thing. Take tonight—there was a fair chance that her ex, Malcolm, would be at the Tavern. Not that she really thought of him much, but it was always awkward to run into him and see the hurt, angry expression in his eyes before he turned his back on her.

It wasn't just about Malcolm, though. Freya wanted more experience and a fresh start.

She would be thirty soon, she reasoned. If she didn't make the move now then she never would.

Deep down, though, she knew she was running away.

It was going to be hard to leave, but for Freya it was simply too hard to stay.

CHAPTER ONE

'IS ANYONE…?'

Freya looked up and quickly realised that the woman in theatre scrubs wasn't asking if she might join Freya at her table in the hospital canteen. Instead all she wanted was one of the spare chairs at Freya's table.

People, Freya thought, didn't even bother to speak in full sentences down here.

'Help yourself.' Freya nodded.

And so the lady did.

It was orientation day at the Primary Hospital, and apart from being asked her name and shown where to go Freya really hadn't spoken to anyone. She had tried during the coffee break, but Rita, the woman she had sat next to during the lectures, had gone off to call her husband.

The schedule had been a full one. First there had been an introduction to the Primary—a large general hospital with a major trauma centre. The volume of patients seen in Casualty per annum was, to Freya, staggering, as was the number of deliveries in Maternity, which had reached seven thousand last year.

There was no such thing as orientation day at Cromayr Bay—a new staff member would be shown around and introduced and made welcome. Here, though, Freya sat with approximately fifty fellow nurses, admin staff and ancillary workers who were commencing, or had just commenced work at the Primary this month alone.

Freya felt like a very small fish in a very large and rather cold sea.

On Friday she had been in to collect her uniforms and her lanyard and had got rather lost on her way out of the huge building. Today, though, sitting in the lecture theatre, she had found out that the red strip painted on the corridor wall led to Casualty and the main exit. So that was good to know. The yellow strip, she had then been told, led to Maternity and the blue to Outpatients.

'It helps not just the staff and the patients,' the admin manager had said, 'but it is also far easier to give directions to visitors. We shall soon be adding a green strip for the Imaging Department. Any more than that and the walls will start to look like rainbows!'

After a morning of lectures and films they had been told to head off for lunch and to be back at one.

There was no coloured strip that led to the canteen, but by following the overhead signs Freya had found it quite easily.

The place had been packed, and Freya had rather wished she had thought to bring her own lunch, as most of her fellow orientation candidates seemed to have done. Perhaps that was why she sat alone.

She hadn't brought any change for the vending machines, so she'd queued up and selected a salad wrap, a packet of cheese and biscuits and a coffee, and then scanned the busy canteen for a table.

They'd all been rather full, but there had been a couple of seats that had seemed free on a table for four.

'Do you mind if I join you?' Freya had asked.

'We're just leaving,' the man there had said.

They had also left their plates, glasses and cups.

She had to stop comparing things to Cromayr Bay, but all this was just so unlike anything she was used to.

Since her father had left her at her one-bedroom flat, four days ago, Freya hadn't really spoken to anyone. Well, apart from a couple of shop assistants and a worker on the Underground who had helped Freya to buy a travel pass.

She had rung her mother and assured her that everything was fantastic.

'Your dad said the flat's a bit grim.'

It *was* rather grim, but Freya had reassured her mum that it was nothing a few rugs and pictures wouldn't pretty up, and reminded her that it was a brilliant location—just a ten-minute walk to the Underground.

'Is anyone…?'

Freya looked up as another unfinished question was asked by an elderly man in a porter's uniform.

'No,' Freya said, and gestured to an empty seat. 'Help yourself.'

He said nothing in response, just took a seat at the table and opened up some sandwiches, then pulled out a newspaper and started to read.

There was no conversation.

Having finished her wrap, Freya peeled open the foil on her cheese and crackers. But she really wasn't hungry so she put them down and pushed away her plate.

Glancing at her phone, she saw that there were still another fifteen minutes left until she was due back.

'Is this seat…?' asked a snooty, deep, but far from unpleasant male voice.

Freya was suddenly sick to the back teeth of unfinished questions.

'Is this seat *what*?' she asked, but as she looked up her indignation took a rapid back seat as she was momentarily sideswiped by six feet plus of good looks dressed in blue theatre scrubs.

He had straight brown hair that was messy, and was so crumpled-looking that, despite the hour, he appeared to have just got out of bed. A stethoscope hung around his neck, and in his hands was a very laden tray.

Freya regretted her brusque response, but consoled herself that he probably hadn't understood a word she had said.

Oh, but he had!

'Is this seat *taken*?' he enquired, more politely, though the smile he wore had a tart edge.

'Please,' Freya said. 'Help yourself.'

He put down the tray, and Freya assumed when he looked around and then wandered off that he must be locating a spare chair for his companion. On his tray there were two mugs of tea, a carton of milk and six little boxes of cereal—the type that her mother had used to get when the family had gone camping, or in the holidays as a treat, when she and her brothers would fight over who got what.

But instead of a chair and a companion he returned with a spoon.

'Len,' he said to the porter by way of greeting. He got a 'humph' in return, but the good-looking stranger didn't seem in the least bothered by the less than friendly response.

As Freya drank her coffee she tried not to look at him, and pretended not to notice when he opened each box of cereal in turn and poured them into the one bowl with all the flavours combined. It was a heap of cornflakes and chocolate puffs and coloured circles, and then he added to his concoction the small carton of milk.

No, there was no companion about to arrive, for next he added sugar to both cups of tea and made light work of the first.

And still Freya tried not to notice.

A domestic came round with a trolley and started to pick up the collection of cereal boxes, as well as the mess that the previous occupants had left in their wake.

'Done?' she asked Freya as she reached for her plate.

'Yes, thank you,' she said, and then blinked as the porter—Len—actually spoke.

'Do you mind?'

'Sorry?' Freya asked as he pointed to her plate.

'You're not going to eat those?' he asked, pointing to the open cheese and crackers that Freya hadn't touched.

'No.'

'Do you mind if I have them?'

'Go ahead,' Freya agreed—because, really, what else could she do?

'Ta very much,' Len said, and took out a piece

of kitchen paper from his pocket and wrapped the cheese and biscuits in them.

The domestic didn't seem in the least perturbed by this odd exchange, and cleared up the boxes and plates. Then as she wheeled her trolley off, The Man Who Liked His Breakfast Cereal, spoke.

'Here you go, Len.' He pushed a granola bar across the table to him.

'Cheers!' Len pocketed his bounty as he stood up and then walked out of the canteen.

Goodness, Freya thought, people here were *so* odd. She simply couldn't imagine asking a complete stranger for the leftover food on their plate.

But then that deep, snooty voice spoke again and attempted to clarify things a little.

'He only talks to the animals.'

'I'm not with you.'

'Len,' he explained. 'He's miserable around people, but he visits an animal shelter in his free time and he's always after treats for them.'

'Oh!' Freya let out a little laugh.

'You're new,' he said, glancing at her lanyard.

He had realised she was staff, but was quite

certain he would have noticed her before if she wasn't new.

She wore a dark shift dress that accentuated her pale bare arms, and her black curly hair was loose and down to her shoulders. From the little he had heard, he guessed she was far from home.

'I'm here for my orientation day,' Freya said.

He grimaced. 'I've done a few of those in my time. The fire lecture, the union rep...'

'We haven't had a fire lecture yet,' Freya said. 'That's this afternoon. I think it's a film, followed by a demonstration.'

'Fun,' he drawled as he rolled his eyes. 'Mind you, I did have a patient who tried to set fire to the ward once...'

She waited for more, but he'd gone back to his cereal.

'Breakfast?' Freya asked.

'And lunch.' He moved on to his second mug of tea. 'Are you new to London as well as the hospital?'

Freya nodded. 'I got here last week.'

'I worked in Glasgow for a while.'

'For how long?'

'A year. I couldn't understand a word anybody said. "Pardon" became my most-used word.'

'I'm having the same problem—although in reverse,' Freya admitted. 'I have to keep repeating myself.'

'I can understand you.'

'Then you're the first.'

'You're not from Glasgow, though?'

She was far too soft spoken for that, he thought. But not soft. He had liked the edge to her tone when he'd asked if the seat was taken. Richard *loved* the challenge of a sullen woman.

'No, I'm from Cromayr Bay.'

'Never heard of it.'

'Fife,' Freya said. 'Overlooking the Firth.'

'Never heard of it,' he said again.

But this time he smiled just a smidge and she couldn't tell if he was teasing.

'How are you finding London?'

'It's early days.' Freya gave a small shrug.

'Ah, after a few late nights you'll come to love it.'

It was then that she noticed his eyes—or rather, it was then that she *properly* noticed them.

In his good-looking face there were several stand-outs. If she'd been describing him to Alison, his sculpted cheekbones and attractive full mouth were two features she might easily have named, and that his hazel eyes were just so much *more* than hazel. They were the colour of burnt amber, with a smatter of golden flecks, and they made Freya feel as if she were gazing upon an open fire.

Or was that more from the way he absolutely held her gaze as she replayed his words in her mind?

'Ah, but after a few late nights you'll come to love it.'

Those words had sounded like an invitation.

As Freya held their eye contact steady, she wasn't quite sure how, but he made her his sole focus.

And he was hers.

Gone was the canteen, and gone too was the noise.

But then he spoke, and Freya found herself blinking at the intrusion of words.

'So, where will you be working?

'Maternity. I'm a midwife. The name's Freya,' she added, and she was not just being polite. His stethoscope was hanging over his lanyard and she wanted to know his name and just who this delectable stranger was.

She would have to wait to find out, though. His pager was trilling. As he looked at it he scooped the last of his cereal into his mouth and then gulped down the remaining tea as he stood.

'I expect you to be fully versed in the operating of a fire extinguisher the next time we meet.'

'I'll do my best,' Freya said, but he had already gone, his large frame moving swiftly through the tables as people made way to let him past.

She watched.

And not idly.

The overhead chimes started then, and Freya heard that the Cardiac Arrest Team was needed in Casualty.

Through the glass windows of the canteen Freya watched as he ran down the corridor, and then she turned her head and surveyed his empty cereal bowl and the two empty cups of tea.

Freya didn't know his name, just that he was

gorgeous. Effortlessly so. And way more gorgeous than *she* could handle.

She hadn't been born yesterday. In fact, Freya's thirtieth birthday was fast approaching. And there was something about him that told her he had learnt to flirt from the cradle. There had certainly been a tease and a flirt in his eyes when they spoke—especially with that little quip about late nights.

Well, there would be no late nights spent with *him*! She was far too guarded and sensible for that.

With her lunch break over, Freya headed back to the lecture theatre for the afternoon session of her orientation day. Sure enough it was the fire lecture. She watched the film and tried not to smile when they were given a demonstration on how to use the various fire extinguishers.

And even as she watched and listened Freya wanted to know more about the time her lunch companion's patient had tried to set fire to the ward.

And she wanted to know his name.

Fully versed in the fire policy at the Primary, as well as in the various codes used for emergencies of different natures, and how to report safety hazards, Freya found that it was time for coffee—and, she guessed, another fifteen minutes of standing alone.

'There's a lot to take in, isn't there?' said Rita, the woman who had earlier been sitting next to her.

'There is,' Freya agreed. 'Where will you be working?'

'I used to be a domestic on Maternity. I'm hoping they'll send me back there, but I haven't been told where I'm going yet. You?'

'I'm a midwife, so I'm *certainly* hoping that they'll be sending me there!' Freya joked.

'Pardon?'

'Maternity,' Freya said instead.

'Well, I hope to see you there.'

They headed back for their final lectures about the pay office and superannuation. Rita took furtive notes and Freya did her level best not to tune out completely.

Finally orientation day was concluded, and the fifty or so new Primary Hospital workers all headed for home.

Freya followed the red line, and sure enough was soon approaching Casualty.

And there he was.

The man who had understood her when she spoke.

He must be hungry again, Freya thought, watching him feed coins into a vending machine.

Gosh, he really was good-looking—and just so tall and broad. Even side-on there was a presence to him. She wondered if she could come up with a witty line about fire extinguishers in the few seconds she'd have before their paths crossed again.

Except she didn't come up with any witty lines, and neither was one needed—because he collected a bottle of water and a bar of chocolate and headed back into Casualty without noticing her at all.

Freya headed towards the Underground, as did seemingly fifty million other people, and stood squashed between them for the four stops to her flat. And surely those same fifty million people were getting off at the same stop, for they all seemed to be herding towards the escalator with her.

She thought of her little purple car at home. The

one that would never have survived the motorway—which was the reason her father had driven her here. And she thought of the short drive from the hospital to her home and the gorgeous view that awaited her there.

'Cheer up love!' called out a man working at a flower stall. 'It might never happen.'

Freya jolted as she realised he was calling out to her.

She walked into her dingy flat and let out a sigh.

The place looked no better for her efforts over the past four days. She had washed down the walls, but really they needed several coats of paint. The curtains she had washed had shrunk, Freya had realised when she'd put them back, and now they didn't properly close, falling a foot short of the floor. And there was an awful picture of a horse and cart that had to come down!

Tomorrow, Freya decided. When she would also get a rug to cover the mustard-coloured carpet, she thought as she headed into the kitchen.

It was even worse than her kitchen at Cromayr Bay.

But it wasn't just the flat that was upsetting her.

Apart from that gorgeous guy at lunchtime she had barely spoken to a soul since she'd arrived here.

It would be better soon, Freya told herself. Once she got to the maternity unit she would start to make friends.

Wouldn't she?

She was starting to think the flower seller had picked up on her mood correctly. 'It' had indeed happened.

Moving here, Freya was sure, had been a mistake.

CHAPTER TWO

'FIONA, CAN YOU go to Labour and Delivery? I mean Freya.'

Freya nodded. She was getting rather used to being called the wrong name by Stella, the associate unit manager.

'Sure.'

'And can you buddy with Kelly?'

Freya had been working there for a fortnight now, and today she was to go to the labour and delivery unit. 'Buddying' meant that she and Kelly would check each other's CTG readings to ensure that two sets of skilled eyes overlooked the tracings. Even after two weeks it was no less daunting than it had been on her first day.

She had spent the first week in the antenatal clinic and the past few days on the maternity ward, and now she was on her second day in L&D.

There were *so* many staff, and each day there seemed to be new faces. Freya had really clicked with one midwife yesterday, but as it had turned out she'd just been doing an agency shift, so Freya had no idea if she would see her again.

Everyone was so busy, and though they were all professional and nice, there just wasn't the same vibe from her colleagues that Freya was used to.

As she walked to L&D Freya rolled over the top of her trousers as they were way too loose. Her uniform consisted of dark blue trousers and a pale blue top and it was less than flattering. She couldn't care less, but the sizing must be off because it hung off her. Although she *had* lost a bit of weight since she'd arrived, due to the constant busy pace and the lack of time to do a proper shop.

As she pressed the green button and the doors to L&D parted she saw a woman pushing an IV, walking the corridor with her support person. Freya gave them a smile.

She checked the board and saw that Dr Mina was the obstetrician in charge today. In the short while she had been at the Primary, Freya had worked with her several times, and found her incredibly efficient as well as a calming presence to the patients.

The hand-over was in depth, so that everyone was well-versed on all the patients—both those present now and those expected to arrive over the course of the shift.

'Freya, can you take over from Angela in D5?' asked Pat, the midwife in charge of L&D today. 'She's awaiting an epidural, but finding an anaesthetist this morning is proving a rather hard ask.'

'Has the second-on been paged?' Freya asked, and that earnt her a wry smile from her colleague.

'*Everyone's* been paged, but there's been a five-car pile-up on the M25 and there was already a dissecting triple A being rushed to Theatre, along with a collapse on the paediatric ward. Then we had to call the Crash Caesarean Team out half an hour ago. Right now Anaesthetics are snowed under, and it's a case of if a patient's screaming then at least they're breathing.'

Freya took a breath of her own. That patient-load sounded like a full week's work in Cromayr Bay at the height of summer, but it was just another morning at the Primary.

Or not. Because then Pat explained that it had been an exceptionally busy night in Casualty too.

'Just remind Kathy in D5 that she hasn't been forgotten. Her husband, Ben, is getting upset.'

Freya checked her patient's details and then went into the delivery suite. The lights were low and the suite was dim, and Kathy was kneeling up and holding on to the head of the delivery bed as Angela pressed a hot pack into her back.

'Hi, there,' Freya said as she approached. 'I'm Freya. I'm—'

'Are you an anaesthetist?' Kathy's husband snapped.

'No, I'm a midwife,'

'Not good enough! My wife has been waiting for two hours for an epidural.'

'Please, Ben,' Kathy implored, but then her face screwed up and she leant on her forearm as a contraction came.

Angela helped her through it as Freya checked all the equipment. Angela brought her up to speed with Kathy's progress, but then gestured with her head to the door. Freya followed her out.

'The husband is getting really tense and it's up-setting Kathy,' Angela said.

'I can see that.' Freya nodded.

'He's a great guy—he's just terrified. But Kathy has still got a good way to go. I've called down to Casualty but two of their patients are currently being transferred to ICU, so they're very tied up. The anaesthetist in our theatre is aware, though he's probably half an hour or so away.'

'Okay…'

'You could try calling Switch and asking—'

'No need.'

A voice she recognised, though she hadn't heard it since her orientation day, caused Freya to turn around.

'Oh, Richard!' Angela sighed in relief. 'Am I pleased to see you.'

'Not as pleased as your patients will be. What room?'

'D5 is first,' Angela said. 'It's all set up for you.'

'Thanks, Angela,' he said. 'Freya.'

She gave him a smile. 'Richard.'

Finally she knew his name.

And, more than that, he was still *stunning*.

He had been wearing scrubs when they'd met, but this morning he wore a dark suit and a crisp white shirt with a silver-grey tie. His straight hair was damp, and rather more in need of a cut than the last time she'd seen him, and he was unshaven.

In seconds she took in every delicious detail, and the last few didn't quite fit. He was so well turned out that the unshaven jaw stood out for Freya.

Instead of heading to the suite, he took the patient's notes and walked over to the desk. The sharp, fresh scent of his cologne lingered. Freya saw him removing his jacket as she followed Angela back into D5.

'Good news,' Angela said. 'The anaesthetist is here.'

'Well, where is he, then?' Ben demanded.

'Dr Lewis is just reading up on the notes.' Angela gave Kathy a lovely smile. 'I shall leave you in Freya's hands. You've been amazing, Kathy.'

Kathy nodded and tried to say goodbye, but was overwhelmed by another contraction. Freya took over, rubbing Kathy's back and trying to establish a rapid bond with the woman, and also with her husband.

'Would you like to come and rub her back?' Freya suggested, but Ben stood against the wall and gave a tense shake of his head.

Yes, it was all terribly different from anything she was used to. Usually Freya would have seen her patients at antenatal clinic, and often their partners too.

'Well done, Kathy,' Freya said as the contraction faded. Knowing that the anaesthetist was here, Freya suggested that Kathy empty her bladder and walked with her, pushing the IV pole, to the en suite bathroom attached to the delivery room.

'He's nervous,' Kathy said, explaining Ben's behaviour.

'Of course he is,' Freya said. 'It's hard work for the women but it's hell on the men.'

That made Kathy laugh a little.

Freya waited outside, and when Kathy came out after washing her hands, she asked Freya a question. 'Do you have children?'

'No.' Freya said. 'I've got nieces and nephews,

and my best friend's expecting, but I'd definitely like my own someday.'

She was actually enjoying getting to know the women here, and opening up to people who didn't know her at all, Freya realised. At home, had she said that, it would have been all around town that she and Malcolm were trying for a baby.

'We tried for ages…' Kathy sighed. 'I thought it would never happen.'

'Well, it clearly is.'

'Thanks, Freya,' Kathy said as Freya pushed the IV pole. But as they got to the door she paused. 'Please…' she said. 'Don't mind Ben. His bark is far worse than his bite.'

'I know that. You'll be feeling a lot more comfortable soon, and I'm sure he will too.'

She was just helping Kathy back onto the delivery bed when the door opened and she saw the beautiful man she now knew was called Richard come in.

'Where the *hell* have you been?' Ben said by way of greeting.

'I'm Dr Lewis,' he responded. 'Consultant anaesthetist.' Then he smiled at his patient. 'Hello, Mrs Hudson.'

But Ben wasn't finished yet. 'She was booked to have an epidural hours ago, but she's been left screaming in pain.'

'I'm aware of that, Mr Hudson, and I agree that it's unfortunate, but I'm here now.'

'It's more than unfortunate, it's not good enough,' he retorted.

'Ben, please...' Kathy pleaded, but her husband still wasn't done.

'Where were you?'

'Actually,' Richard said as he rolled up his sleeves, 'I was in bed when I was called to see if I could come in. I'm not supposed to be here until eight.'

It was only just after seven. And Freya understood now why he hadn't shaved.

'Now...' He looked over to his patient as he tied on a plastic apron. 'Would you prefer me to call you Mrs Hudson or Kathy?'

'Kathy.'

'Well, Kathy, we'll have you feeling a lot more comfortable soon.'

He was very meticulous. As Freya helped Kathy to sit on the edge of the bed for the procedure Richard Lewis went through all that had been set up. He made no small talk as he checked and re-checked everything.

'Right,' he said, as if to himself, and then he addressed Kathy. 'You're going to feel a sting from the local anaesthetic and then a bit of pressure. I'll need you to stay as still as you can—do you understand that?'

'I do—but what if I get a contraction.'

'It's fine. I'm used to them. I'll work around it.'

He went through everything that she could expect to feel, and as the next contraction came he put on gloves, waiting for the pain to diminish before the procedure commenced.

'I'm sorry,' Ben said suddenly.

'It's fine,' Richard responded. 'It's awful to see someone you love in pain. However, by all accounts your partner has been doing marvellously. Let's try and make this last bit a whole lot easier for her, shall we?'

Whoa! Freya thought as she held on to Kathy.

He had somehow accepted the apology while reminding the husband just who this day was about.

'Why don't you come this side?' Freya suggested to Ben. She knew he was really just terribly anxious. 'You can hold Kathy's hand.'

This time he didn't shake his head and came and took his wife's hand.

Richard worked quietly and soon the epidural was in. Kathy lay back on the delivery bed.

'You'll need to stay in bed now,' Richard reminded her as he disposed of his sharps and then removed his gloves. 'Thank you, Freya. Can I leave my mess to you? I believe I'm wanted in D3.'

'Sure.'

Freya checked Kathy's obs, and those of the baby, and by the time she had tidied up Kathy was indeed starting to feel the benefits of the epidural.

'You should try and get a little rest now,' Freya suggested. 'I'll be in and out, and there's the call bell if you have any concerns at all.'

'Freya!'

Her name was called the second she stepped out of the room. 'Can you go and take the baby in D7?'

Freya nodded and headed to delivery suite number seven. 'Taking' a baby was wonderful indeed. It combined all the joy with barely a hint of the pain.

Stepping in to the delivery suite, she found the atmosphere was lovely and peaceful. Kelly, one of the other midwives was there, along with the soon-to-be father, who had his arms wrapped around his wife's shoulders.

In fact Kelly was so calm that even when she told Freya that Dr Mina and the anaesthetist had been paged she did it in such an open way that there was no jolt of alarm from the mother.

'The baby is small for the dates and the head is smaller than expected,' she said, and Freya checked all the equipment was ready.

Despite the unexpectedly small head, everything seemed to be under control.

'Try not to push, Sita,' Kelly said. 'Just pant.'

'Okay,' Sita said, and fought against the urge.

'Good girl,' said Kelly. Her focus was totally on the delivery, and she didn't look over when the door opened.

'Hello, there,' Richard said quietly, and Kelly calmly told him the reason for him being paged.

'Thirty-seven weeks and small for dates,' Kelly explained.

The room was getting crowded. Stella had come in after Richard, followed by Dr Mina just as the head was delivered. And now there was Guy Masters, the paediatrician on call, whom Freya had already met.

'Well done, Sita,' Dr Mina said. 'Just breathe and do as Kelly says. Dr Masters is a paediatrician and he's here to check your baby.'

The head really was tiny, and Freya found she was holding her breath as the body slithered out. But even as she accepted him he started to cry. His huge eyes were blinking at the light and his little face was wrinkled.

He was utterly gorgeous, Freya thought as she held this tiny piece of the future in her hands. Tiny, but perfect. And as she rubbed him down Guy was already examining him.

'One that is better out than in,' Guy said.

The baby had clearly not been getting sufficient

nutrition in-utero, but he was angry and defiant and utterly perfect.

'I don't think we need you, Richard,' he said as loud cries pierced the room and the baby pinked up beautifully.

'Not with those lungs,' Richard agreed. And it was just as well he wasn't needed because his pager was going off.

He left unnoticed by all, Freya thought. All except her.

'I think he's ready to meet his mum,' Guy said, and Freya popped a little hat on the baby to keep him warm, wrapped him, then carried him over to his waiting parents.

She smiled as she watched a family being born. Freya loved delivering babies, but *taking* them was special too. They always tried to deliver them straight to the mother, but sometimes, as with this unexpected small size, the baby needed a proper examination. Apart from his size this one was doing just fine. Another perfect new life.

The day seemed to be running away from her. Busy, a bit crazy, and after her hectic morning she could only take a coffee break on the run at the desk.

There, Dr Mina was speaking with Richard and Kelly was chatting with Stella about a film they were going to see at the weekend.

'It's supposed to be really good,' Freya commented, subtly fishing to be asked to go with them, but Kelly just nodded her head.

Freya took her lunch in the staff room, and just as she returned she was told that Kathy was ready to push.

When she got to the delivery room Ben was white with fear and Freya gave him a smile.

'I thought you'd gone home,' Ben said.

'And miss out on this?' Freya asked.

Ben proved to be a champion when it came to coaxing Kathy to push. It was clearly an excellent epidural, because she could feel the sensation and some pressure but had no pain.

'Another big push,' Freya encouraged. 'Come on—a really big one, right down into your bottom.'

This time it was Kelly who arrived to take the baby and soon Freya delivered a chunky baby boy.

He was gorgeous, and there were tears from both Ben and Kathy as he lay on her stomach, blinking at the world.

'Are you going to cut the cord, Dad?' Kelly asked, and Ben came over with tears in his eyes to have that special moment with his son.

Baby Hudson didn't have a name yet, but by the time Freya was ready for home he'd had his first feed and Kathy had had a well-earned cup of tea.

It hadn't been a particularly busy day, or so Freya had been told, and yet she was exhausted.

The high of Baby Hudson's birth lasted right through the Tube journey, but faded as she began the walk for home.

Freya had never been surrounded by more people, and yet she had never felt more alone.

There was a social club at the hospital, but she was hardly going to walk in on her own, and making friends was proving a lot more difficult than she had anticipated.

However, later, rather than sit alone with her noodles, Freya reminded herself that she did indeed have friends and called Alison.

'How are things?' Alison asked.

'Busy,' Freya said. 'Well, work is—the social life, not so much.'

'But you're in *London*!' Alison said.

'I know...' Freya sighed, because Alison's observation just made it worse. 'I *am* trying,' she admitted. 'I sort of hinted to a couple of girls at work that there was a film I'd like to see, but I felt like a bent coin in a vending machine.'

'Rejected?' Alison laughed.

'Exactly.'

'Keep at it. Just say yes to anything you're invited to.'

'I'll have to be invited somewhere first.'

'You *will* be.'

'How are *you*?' Freya asked. She felt her throat clamp tight, but she swallowed and pushed through, trying to keep her voice casual and light. 'How's the baby.'

'All good. I'm fifteen weeks now, and I swear I've got a bump, although Callum says it's too early.'

Freya hesitated, because women sometimes showed more quickly with a second pregnancy, but she couldn't gauge whether or not that was the right thing to say to Alison now.

Freya dealt with pregnant woman every working day, and she dealt with loss too. And, what was more, she prided herself on dealing with it well. Yet when it came to her friend she felt like an absolute novice, and simply didn't know how to be around the subject of Alison's pregnancy.

Freya was terrified she might break down, and Alison didn't need that. Of course they had both cried together in the days following Andrew's birth, and then his death, but right now Freya was sure it was time to be strong.

'When's your ultrasound?' Freya asked.

'In two weeks' time. I'll believe it's really happening once I've heard its little heart.'

Alison's voice broke then, and Freya closed her eyes when she heard it. 'It will be okay,' she offered.

'You don't *know* that, Freya,' Alison snapped.

'I know, but…' Her voice trailed off.

'Sorry,' Alison said.

'Don't be.'

And then Freya turned on her midwife voice

and said all the right things, just as she would to a patient.

But Alison was her best friend. It was awkward and it was difficult and things were different between them.

There was no escaping that.

CHAPTER THREE

RICHARD LEWIS REALLY was stunning.

Even asleep he managed to bring a little skip to Freya's heart when she walked in and saw him, lying across several chairs in the staff room.

Pat and Kelly were deep in conversation there, and didn't seem bothered in the least by the sight of Richard sprawled out.

It bothered Freya—or rather it bothered her senses. She tried not to peek as she stirred her soup, but she didn't try very hard because her eyes kept wandering over.

He hadn't shaved again, and Freya knew he must have been working all night. It was now late morning.

She had been at the Primary for a month now, and he was no less intriguing and no less gorgeous.

During the course of her working week Freya

saw him regularly. He had a new registrar, who wasn't yet able to do epidurals unsupervised, so Richard was in L&D quite often to oversee his work. And he was always called if there was a difficulty with a delivery or a Caesarean.

There was rarely time for conversation, though.

Freya considered the Maternity Unit here extremely busy, but *his* workload was incredible. He rushed to emergencies all over the hospital— and that was aside from Theatre and patients in the ICU.

Of course there were many anaesthetists in such a busy hospital, but Freya, despite her warnings to herself, was only interested in one!

Her instincts had been right. He was a heartbreaker, indeed. She had found that out from the other midwives. Not that they'd actually confided in her! No—she was still struggling to fit in. But she had overheard a couple of conversations, and apparently he'd just ended a brief fling with a nurse in Casualty. And Von, one of the other midwives, was *still* hoping that she and Richard might get back together.

She looked over at him. He needed a shave and a

haircut. Or rather *he* might think that if he looked in the mirror, but to Freya he looked just fine.

Better than fine!

He was like a bear, Freya thought. Not a fat bear, more like a bear just out of hibernation, all slender and restless and hungry.

And then she smiled at her mad thoughts.

Pat was chatting to Kelly about the film that Freya *still* hadn't seen. 'I was thinking I might go this weekend,' Pat said.

'You *have* to,' said Kelly. 'It's amazing.'

Freya again tried to be brave. 'I'm dying to see it,' she admitted.

'You should.' Kelly looked over and nodded, and then she stood. 'Come on, Pat. We'd better get back.'

Once they'd gone Freya let out a sigh. Over and over she'd been mentioning that she'd love to go and see the film, but there had been no takers. How much more of a hint was she supposed to give?

She sat staring at the television and took a sip of her revolting packet soup. And then a voice—

one she had really come to like—chimed deep and low.

'I'll take you to the bloody film.'

She looked over.

'I can take a hint.'

'Sorry?'

'You keep suggesting it every time I'm near. All you have to do ask.'

'I wasn't hinting for *you* to take me!' Freya said, and actually found herself going red. 'I was waiting for one of *them* to ask me along.'

'You're too subtle,' he said, and lay there smiling at her. 'Poor Freya-no-Friends.'

'Don't!' she said, but she was smiling.

'You have to invite yourself—or just go along with them.'

'What? Just turn up? Like a stalker?'

'Well, maybe not.'

'I've *always* had friends,' Freya said, for she had been giving it some considerable thought. 'But I've realised that's because we all grew up together. I've never actually had to *make* any.'

'Rubbish,' he scoffed. 'You're saying that because you grew up in a village you all get along?'

'It's not a village.'

'Well, town or whatever,' he said. 'But I'm sure there are people you don't like there. You're not automatically friends with everyone you grew up with. God, I loathed Derek next door, and we had to play together all the time.'

'Why?'

'That's for another time.'

He stretched and yawned and sat up, more bear-like than ever as he gave himself a sort of shake.

'I'm starving,' he said.

'I've got some soup.'

'No, thanks.' Richard pulled a face. 'I'm going to head down to the canteen. What time do you finish?'

She'd thought he must have been joking about going out. 'Not until nine.'

'Well, I'm covering for Simon until eight, so I doubt I'll get away much before then. I'll meet you at the entrance to Casualty.'

'I don't even know if the film's on,' Freya said. 'Or the session time.'

'Times,' he corrected. 'It's on everywhere.

You're not in Cromayr Bay now, where they have to come and change the reels…'

He was teasing, yet it made her laugh. 'It's not *that* bad.'

'Give me your number and if I can I'll text you if I'm not going to make it. But if I'm not there by a quarter past, just head for home. It'll mean I'm stuck somewhere—nothing else. I won't be avoiding you!'

He even turned the subject of her being a little lonely into a smile.

'I'll look forward to it,' Freya said, and recited her number. 'And, no, I won't be upset if…' she started, but her voice trailed off as Stella came in.

'Freya, I know you're not due back yet, but we've got a bit of a rush on.'

'Of course,' Freya said, and she stood and finished the last of her soup, a little surprised when Richard spoke again.

'I'll see you around nine, then?'

Freya felt her cheeks were a little warm as she walked back round to the unit—because he had made it clear in front of Stella that they were meeting up tonight.

It meant nothing, she told herself. It was just two colleagues going out. If it had been Kelly or Pat or anyone else she wouldn't be giving it too much thought and Stella was surely the same.

'See Rose?' Stella said, and pointed over to Rita, the domestic who had done her orientation with Freya on her first day.

'Rita,' Freya corrected as they walked.

'Rita, then.' Stella nodded. 'See how it looks like she's emptying the rubbish…?'

'Er…yes,' Freya answered.

'Well, she's not—she's actually collecting all the discarded hearts…'

Freya pressed her lips together as she realised what Stella meant, and even managed a wry smile as Stella spoke on.

'Oh, look, she's going under the bed. Must have found another one. You know how he dashes from one emergency to another?' She didn't await Freya's response. 'Well, he's the same with women.'

'Stella.' Freya stopped walking and gave her senior a wide smile—because she knew his reputation and because Stella had made her smile. 'We're going to the cinema. No more, no less.'

'Don't say I didn't warn you.'

It was a slow evening by Primary Hospital standards, which would have meant a chaotic one back home! But by nine Freya was in the changing room. She took her phone from her locker, as she chose not to have it on her at work, and found herself letting out a breath of relief that there was no text from Richard to say he couldn't make it.

And then she swallowed, because relief possibly wasn't the right word.

Freya was nervous about tonight.

She so wanted to make friends.

Only this didn't feel like any friendship Freya had ever known!

She pulled off her horrible uniform, changed into the grey linen dress and ballet pumps she had worn into work and let her hair down, pulling her curls out with her fingers.

In the end it was actually Freya who was a little late, and when she arrived at the entrance to Casualty he was checking his phone.

He was out of scrubs and in a suit, although minus a tie, and beside him Freya felt rather drab.

She looked far from drab, though. In fact, Richard thought as she walked towards him, she was wearing the same dress she had been on the day they had met.

And that was concerning, because usually he couldn't recall what any woman had worn the previous night, let alone in previous weeks. He'd even joked to a friend that he'd be hell at reporting a missing person because he'd be unable to tell the police what the missing person was wearing.

He didn't really notice such things, other than thinking, *Oh, she looks nice.*

With Freya though he'd be able to describe in detail to any police officer that the dress was grey linen, and it was a touch looser than it had been on the day they had met.

Yes, Officer, she had on black pumps and no stockings, just pale slender legs. And her hair was worn down. It didn't actually sit on her shoulders since it's too curly for that, it just holds its wild shape there. And she has green eyes, Officer, and soft full lips.

Anything else? the officer would ask.

Well, she's been a bit lonely since she arrived here, he would say. *I didn't give it too much thought at the time...*

But he was giving it some serious thought now.

Not that he showed his concern. Richard, thanks to his job, was incredibly good at that.

'Right,' he said as they headed out onto the street. 'The film is on at ten, so if we skip all the trailers we'll have time to go and get something decent to eat. I am sick of eating on the run.'

'That sounds brilliant.'

'Are you on in the morning?' he asked.

Freya nodded.

'And me.'

And then Freya was delivered another thinly veiled warning as Stella dashed past them to a car in which presumably her husband had come to meet her. 'Enjoy *the film*, Freya!'

'I will,' Freya called back.

'Has she been telling tales about me?' Richard asked as they walked out onto the street.

'No!'

The street was busy enough that it could have

been a Saturday during the day back home, and she was glad it was dark enough that he'd hopefully missed her blush as she lied.

'Of course she has,' Richard said. 'And they're all true.'

'Then it's a good job we're just heading out to see a film,' Freya said.

'Indeed.'

But first they would eat…

'Is Italian okay?' he checked, and she nodded as he led them to a very lovely casual-looking restaurant, tucked away from the main street.

Freya only realised just how hungry she was as the gorgeous scents inside hit her, and they were guided to a table looking out onto the street.

'Can I get you some drinks to start?' the waiter offered.

'Freya?' Richard asked.

'Just water.'

'And me,' Richard said. 'Sparkling?'

'Lovely,' Freya agreed.

The menu was delectable, and she decided on a creamy carbonara, while Richard settled for *osso bucco.*

'So,' he said when their order was in, 'how are you finding it at the Primary?'

'It's fine,' Freya said, and she saw his eyes narrow. 'Well, it's a bit overwhelming. I expected it to be busy, of course, but I didn't realise it would be quite so full-on.'

'What was it like where you worked before?'

'I was in a birthing centre attached to a hospital. We saw the mothers for all their antenatal care, then right up to the postnatal check.'

'How many deliveries at the centre?' Richard asked.

'About a hundred a year. So it's been a big change for me to come somewhere that averages more than that in a week. Still, I wanted the experience.'

'You could have got that more locally,' Richard said, tearing open a bread roll. 'The Women's Hospital in Edinburgh surely delivers a similar amount?'

'Yes,' Freya agreed. 'I did a stint there during my training. But I wanted something completely different, and it was sort of now or never.'

'Are your parents back home?'

'And my brothers.' Freya nodded.

'Do you all get on?' he asked, because despite himself he wanted to know more. Surely there must be more of a reason she had left—not just in her work, but her home, friends and family too?

'Oh, yes. I've got my own place, but I see plenty of them. The older brother, though they're both younger than me, has got two children. I delivered the younger one.'

'I can't imagine having a sister-in-law, let alone being that close to her.'

'Don't you have siblings?' Freya asked.

'No, there's just me.'

'And are you from London?'

'Kent.'

'Do you get back there much?'

'Now and then,' Richard said, and then he hesitated.

He rarely spoke about his family, but he felt no sense of her probing beyond what he was comfortable with, and actually he found it was nice to sit and chat.

'I see my father sometimes, and my mother's here in London. She's just got engaged.' He

rolled his eyes, just as their meals were delivered.
'Again.'

Then came the pepper grinder, and the parmesan cheese, and he thought certainly they would speak about the food now, or the film they were about to see—or even, as Richard usually would, get on with flirting. And yet he was still curious to hear more about her.

'Do you miss your old job?'

'Yes and no,' Freya said. 'I was often delivering the babies of people I'd been to school with, or their wives. And I know a lot of people around town. And while it's nice knowing your patients...'

He nodded. 'My father's a GP. I know only too well the downside. He was never off duty—even going out for a meal like this he'd be interrupted. The only time I remember him getting away from work was if we went on holiday, and even then patients would call him for advice.'

'I don't mind that so much,' Freya admitted.

Her dismissal of the intrusion aspect of things surprised him.

'It's more the fact of everyone knowing everyone else's business,' she explained. 'And of course when a pregnancy goes wrong it's much harder.'

'It's just part of the job,' Richard said.

'Yes, but it's more difficult when you know the patient.'

'Perhaps…'

To Freya, he didn't sound as if he necessarily agreed. 'There's no *perhaps* about it.'

He opened his mouth to say something, but then changed his mind. It had been a very long day, and they were here to relax after all.

Still, there was something he really would like to know. 'Was there a break-up involved?' he asked.

'Sorry?'

'Is that the reason you left—is there an ex-Mr Freya back home…'

'No!' She laughed. 'I've never been married, but I did break up with someone earlier in the year. It really didn't have anything to do with my decision to leave, though.'

'Are you sure?' Richard frowned through disbelieving eyes.

She was very guarded and, although they were

chatting easily, he sensed she was being prudent in her responses.

For once he wanted to dig for the truth from a woman.

'Well, it might have had *some* influence on it,' she admitted reluctantly. 'There's nothing much worse than going into a pub or a restaurant and knowing there's a pretty good chance that your ex will be there. It was a bit messy, I guess.'

'Who ended it?'

'Me,' Freya said. 'We'd been together for ages and I just…' She didn't want to talk about Alison's baby and the pregnancy that had gone wrong. But it had been that which had heralded the end for her and Malcolm. 'I was going through a bit of a tough time and he didn't help matters…' She gave a thin smile. 'And so, before even the very curl of his hair started to irk me, I ended it. I guess he wasn't the love of my life.'

'There's no such thing,' Richard declared. 'Work is the only love of my life and I intend to remain faithful to that.'

'How do you do it?' Freya asked. 'I know how

wrung out *I* feel after an emergency, and yet you deal with them each day.'

'It's my oxygen,' Richard said. 'There's nothing I'd rather be doing. Although,' he admitted, 'I don't want to end up like my father. There has to be a balance. I go away a lot on my days off — try to get well away from the hospital.' He gave a tight smile. 'I have some choices that need to be made.'

'Such as…?'

He gave a small shake of his head that told her not to go there. And when she didn't push for more information Richard could have reached over and kissed her there and then.

He didn't, of course, but the thought was there as their eyes locked.

Freya felt the heat spread over her cheeks as their eyes held, and yet she did not tear her gaze away.

God, he was good, Freya thought, for he turned her on without so much as a touch.

And despite her insistence that tonight was about nothing more than seeing a film, she was now heeding Stella's warnings.

It had been lust at first sight, she knew.

And she would not be acting on it.

Freya wasn't like that. One boyfriend at the end of school and throughout her nursing training. A gap of two years and then Malcolm.

A fling with a sexy anaesthetist was so *not* something Freya would do. And it *would* be a fling, for he'd warned her—was warning her right now—that everything she'd heard about him was true.

So she reached for her water and tried to think of something to say as she peeled her mind away from sex.

Because that was all it would be.

Sex.

Ah, but it would be sex with *him*.

'So your mother's engaged?' Freya asked. 'Again?'

He knew she was changing the subject.

Although they were speaking about his family, their minds had just been on sex. He wanted to feel her hair…he wanted to delve into those mixed message eyes.

She almost scalded him with a look, and behind the walls she'd put up there lurked desire.

And he liked her odd sullen moments, interspersed by the brightness of her smile.

But, no, this was not what she needed.

He might have a well-deserved reputation, but he wasn't an utter bastard.

Freya was by her own admission a little lonely, a touch overwhelmed, and he would not be meddling with that pretty head.

So, back to her question. He had to think for a moment what it was. Ah, yes, the many loves of his mother's life.

'My mother is about to enter into her fourth marriage. My father isn't quite so bad. He's only been married and divorced twice. I doubt he'll be taking that step again.' He gave a tight smile. 'Thank God! It really is hard coming up with a new speech each time.'

'Her *fourth*!'

He nodded. 'She left us when I was fifteen, and I'm now thirty-three, so it's not quite as bad as it sounds.' He saw her wide eyes. 'Well, maybe it is. My mother is high-end drama and she just wasn't cut out to be the wife of a country GP. She loathed it. And since she broke up with my father—'

He went quiet, for the first time since they had met. And then…

'Freya?' he said.

'Yes?'

'We've missed the film.'

'Oh!'

She looked around the restaurant and noticed the other diners were thinning out, and then she glanced at her phone. It was coming up for eleven.

'Do you want dessert or coffee?' he offered.

'No, no…' She shook her head.

He walked her to the Underground station and there, she assumed, they would go their separate ways.

'I'll see you home,' he said, when she told him where it was.

'It's only four stops,' Freya protested—but not too much. She still wasn't quite used to the Tube, and she did feel a bit nervous at night. It would be nice to have company.

Or rather it would be nice to have *his* company.

'We're here,' Freya said as they arrived at her flat.

'Well, I'm sorry you didn't get to see your film.'

Freya wasn't sorry.

'It's fine,' she said, toying with whether or not to ask him in and deciding that it would be foolish at best. There was a kiss in the air—she could feel it—and as she looked up at him she wondered how that gorgeous unshaven jaw would feel pressed hard against hers.

'Well, another time, then,' Richard said, resisting the urge to kiss her against the wall.

She wanted a friend, he reminded himself. No more than that.

'Thanks for a nice night. It was good to…' She gave a shrug. 'Well, it was nice not to be talking about babies.'

'All work and no play?' Richard said.

'Something like that.'

She took out her key and he watched as she put it into the lock. That was the difference with Freya—she didn't stand there awaiting his kiss. She didn't seem to want the complication of *them* either.

And yet there was want.

It was a sultry summer night that deserved to end in bed, but Richard was behaving himself.

'Night, Freya.'

'Night, Richard.'

She walked inside, closed the door behind her and leant against it, taking a long breath in.

Had there been a double-lock she would have turned it. Instead she made do with the security chain.

But only to keep herself in.

There was a kiss waiting on the other side of that door—she was sure of it.

And not just a kiss.

Who was she kidding?

It hadn't been a kiss in the air out there—it had been *sex*.

But a fling with Richard Lewis would be foolish at best. Freya didn't do that type of thing. And it *would* be a fling—she knew that. He'd as good as told her so himself.

She told herself that she could never regret a sensible decision. That in the morning she would wake up and be delighted that she'd avoided the awkwardness that would have surely followed.

Except in the morning Freya didn't feel delighted.

She only felt regret.

CHAPTER FOUR

'HOW WAS THE FILM?' Stella asked as Freya walked with her from the changing room.

'Great,' Freya answered. 'It's well worth seeing.'

She was saved from further questioning as the overhead chimes went off, summoning the Trauma Team to Casualty.

She certainly wasn't about to tell Stella that they'd never actually made it to the cinema, as she knew Stella would just read more into it than there had been.

It was unusually quiet, so Freya took the lull in proceedings as a chance to check stock. She had just pulled out the suction catheters and was ticking the order form when the overhead chimes went off again.

They were a common occurrence in a busy hospital such as this, but the summons that came was one that Freya hadn't yet heard.

'Obstetrics Squad to Casualty.'

Freya wasn't a part of the Obstetrics Squad. She had been told about it during her interview, though. Each Maternity shift, a senior midwife carried a pager and would attend to any obstetric emergency elsewhere in the hospital, along with an obstetrician and anaesthetist.

New staff had to attend at least three off-unit emergencies as an observer, and then Dr Mina had to approve them before they were made a part of that team. But just because she wasn't part of the team it didn't mean that there was nothing for Freya to do.

She ran down to the equipment room and opened up the door, and was pulling out the emergency trolley as Stella and Kelly came running from opposite directions.

'Dr Mina's already down there,' Stella informed Kelly, who held the pager for the Obstetrics Squad today. 'Freya, go and observe.'

Freya nodded. She was nervous about this role, yet keen for the experience.

The chimes were pinging again.

'Here...'

It was Len the porter, who had caught up and took over the other side of the trolley, allowing Kelly to run on ahead.

There was everything that might be required, including a neonatal cot, even though there would be one in Emergency. The trolley was set up for any eventuality.

As she swept into Casualty, Freya acknowledged that she was nervous but consoled herself that she was just there to observe. Even if she never made the team it would be good experience for when she went back to Cromayr Bay.

When.

There was no time to dwell on that word, though it jolted her.

Richard was at the head of one of the resuscitation beds and only briefly glanced up when she came in.

'Next bed,' he said, clearly knowing that she wouldn't have been down there before. He gestured with his head to a curtained area beside him, from behind which came the sound of equipment and people, and above all that the screams of a woman.

They were terrified screams and the woman sounded in pain.

'Thanks.' Freya stepped in and saw there was organised chaos taking place.

Dominic, his registrar, was at the head of the bed and the trauma team were around the woman. So too was Dr Mina, tiny in green scrubs and yet authoritative all the same.

She had a Doppler on the woman's stomach and there was the sound of a rapid heartbeat.

'Stay back and observe,' Kelly said. 'You'll be doing this yourself soon.'

There wasn't actually room for her to do anything *but* observe.

An older woman dressed in scrubs was talking to the patient. 'You're okay, Louise,' she said in an Irish brogue. 'We're taking care of you now...'

Louise had on a hard collar, and from what Freya could make out she had been involved in a high-impact motor vehicle accident. There was blunt trauma to her chest and abdomen as well as a head injury.

And she was twenty-six weeks pregnant.

'Louise.' Kelly moved near the head of the bed. 'Your baby has a strong heartbeat…'

But nothing would calm the woman. Louise Eames was absolutely terrified and perhaps, after her head injury, confused too.

There were also concerns that she had abdominal bleeding.

'I'm May, the Unit Manager in this madhouse.' The Irish woman stepped back and spoke to Freya as Kelly took over reassuring the patient. 'I'm a midwife myself. All looks well but, as you know, pregnant women can mask symptoms. I'm worried that she's worse than her observations are showing.'

It was nice to be talked through it all. Most of it Freya knew, but she hadn't actually seen the Obstetrics Squad in action.

'I've told NICU to hold a cot, in case she has to be delivered.' May said. 'Here's Richard now.'

Richard spoke for a moment with Dominic, and then Dominic stepped out—Freya guessed to take over the patient in the next bed.

'Hello, Louise.'

He spoke as if they had already met, Freya

thought. There was just something so reassuring about his voice.

'I'm Dr Lewis, Consultant Anaesthetist.'

Louise screamed again.

'No,' he said. 'No screaming. Save that oxygen for your baby. Now, I want to have another listen to your chest.'

'That's a good girl,' Kelly said to Louise, who was quietening down—though that wasn't necessarily a good sign.

'We're going to get her round for a CT,' Dr Mina said. She and Richard discussed sedation, but Louise seemed a lot calmer now.

The CT was swift, and showed a small tear on Louise's spleen, but everything looked fine with the baby.

'Louise.' Dr Mina spoke to her. 'The hard collar can come off now and you'll be more comfortable. The baby is doing well, but we're going to move you now to the Intensive Care Unit, so that we can keep a close eye on both of you.'

'Will my baby be okay?' It was all Louise wanted to know.

'Everything is looking fine for now,' Dr Mina

said. 'But, Louise, if we need to deliver you, then we will.'

ICU was all ready and waiting, and absolutely the right place for Louise to be.

Freya listened as May gave a detailed handover to the Critical Care Nurse. It was scary for Louise to be there, no doubt, but after the noise of Emergency it was certainly a lot calmer here.

'Thank you,' Dr Mina said to the midwifery staff as they gathered up their equipment to leave.

Richard didn't look up as he was already with another patient and completely focussed.

God, what a job he had, Freya thought as they headed out.

'Poor thing,' Kelly said, as they made their way back, but then she moved straight on to business. 'We'll have to check the trolley as soon as we get back,' she told Freya. 'Just in case we're called again.'

'I hope we're not,' Freya said.

But hope didn't work.

Just after three the chimes went off again. Freya was taking a baby for Pat when she heard them, and they didn't even share a glance—instead they focussed on the little life coming into the world.

Working at The Primary was, Freya thought as she came out of the delivery suite, just all so *intense.*

'Were the chimes for Louise?' Freya asked Stella, who was writing up the board against a background of screams from a woman in the bathroom.

'Yes.' Stella nodded. 'Maternal compromise.'

And then there was paperwork—so much paperwork—only today Freya used it as an excuse and a reason for lingering at the nursing station until well after four, when Kelly came back.

She was wearing a pink theatre cap and still somehow brimming with energy as she and Stella commenced restocking the emergency trolley.

'Mum dropped her blood pressure. Thankfully they were straight onto her. The baby's out.'

He was doing well for dates, but it was Louise that was the main concern. The small tear on her spleen had extended and, as Dr Mina had explained, the signs of hypovolemia were more subtle in pregnancy.

Freya was utterly exhausted as she made her way home.

'Cheer up, love, it might never happen,' said the flower seller, and Freya managed not to shoot him a look.

She stepped into her flat and just flopped onto the couch—lay there staring at the peeling paint on the ceiling, feeling utterly wrung out. Every second at work she felt as if she were on a roller coaster that didn't allow time for catching her breath, or time to reflect.

Poor Louise… She'd been incredibly well taken care of—Freya knew that—but it was all so different from everything she was used to.

Which was what she had wanted, of course. And she was certainly getting experience. But it was draining her.

Stella had told her there would be a case follow-up for Louise, in which Dr Mina would go into greater detail, and Freya was truly grateful that she'd been sent down to Casualty to observe. She really was gaining experience, and if ever a mother came into Cromayr Bay with blunt force trauma…

Freya halted herself there, but it was too late. She knew in that moment that she was imagining herself back at home, just as she had this morning.

But she wasn't *just* here to gain experience. If she'd wanted that, as Richard had pointed out, she could have gained it rather more locally.

No, she had *moved* to London.

Freya hauled herself to the shower and then, having pulled on a robe, surveyed the contents of her fridge.

There wasn't much. She had meant to stop and pick up a few things on her way home. Now she had neither the energy nor the enthusiasm to go out again.

A knock on the door had her padding down the hall—she guessed it would be her neighbour, as their post got muddled on occasion.

Instead it was an unexpected sight for sore eyes. *Richard.*

He'd had a haircut and was clean-shaven. And he was wearing a suit, but no tie, and he looked incredibly tired but still breathtakingly handsome.

'What are you doing here?' Freya asked.

He tried not to notice that she wore only a robe and that her hair was wet as he answered. 'We have a film to see.'

CHAPTER FIVE

'STELLA ASKED ME earlier if I'd enjoyed it...' said Richard.

'She asked me too.' Freya smiled. 'What did you say?'

'I said it was very good, and then I had the awful feeling I was going to be questioned further, but thankfully she had to rush off...'

'Yes, it's been one helluva day,' Freya said. 'How's Louise?'

'Critical.'

'I'm not a reporter, Richard. You can tell me how she really is.'

'She's very unstable. She's had a splenectomy and a Caesarean and has been given a lot of blood. It's going to be a very long night for her.'

'Poor thing.' She was about to let him in, but then she shook her head. 'To be honest, I'm not really in the mood to go out.'

'Fair enough.' Few women refused him, but he found it was rather refreshing. Richard liked her ways.

'We'll do the film another time, maybe?'

'Sure.'

Freya looked at him. He was a man she could never keep, but that didn't matter now. For in her heart Freya knew she would be leaving London soon.

'You can come in,' Freya said. 'If you want to.'

And Richard did want to.

He came through the door and Freya could feel his eyes on her bottom as she led him down the hallway.

His eyes *were* on her bottom—for a moment—but then he looked at the trail of moisture her hair had left on her robe, and then he looked down to her long, bare legs.

He didn't notice the mustard carpet, nor the curtains hanging too short, he simply noticed *her*. As he had from the very first day they had met.

They faced each other, and the want that had been there for a long time, certainly on the doorstep last night, seemed to have followed them into her flat.

'I'll go and get dressed.'

Please don't, Richard thought, but didn't say.

As if she could hear him Freya looked up into his eyes.

'If you disappear on me, at least I'll know what to tell the police,' he said.

'Sorry?'

'She was wearing a pale robe…'

'Oh.'

Freya didn't really understand, but there was a smoky edge to his voice, and as he further explained their eyes locked.

'I don't usually notice what women wear—well, not to the extent that I do with you.'

This morning Freya had regretted her sensible decision last night not to invite him in. Now she wanted to be reckless.

Richard felt as if he could see the barriers between them tumbling down before his eyes. And, yes, desire *did* reside behind her green gaze.

'What else was this woman in a pale robe wearing?' Freya asked. 'Slippers?'

'No,' Richard said, his eyes never leaving hers. For he had already seen her painted toes. 'Her feet were bare and her hair was damp...' His hand came up and he picked up a heavy coil of black hair, as he had ached to do from day one. 'And,' he added, 'I'm quite sure she didn't have any underwear on...'

He watched her mouth part in a smile and lust punched like a fist as they teased and flirted and turned each other on.

'I wish you hadn't shaved,' she whispered as his mouth came to hers.

And then she changed her mind, because instead of rough kisses she got the tang of cologne and Richard's clean-shaven cheek against hers.

'Smooth can be good,' he told her as his hand slid behind her neck.

Her skin flared beneath his fingers and the feel of his cheek had her mouth searching for his.

But then he spoke. 'Freya...'

She frowned at the slight hesitation in his voice, for it was unfamiliar. He was always, *always* so confident and direct.

Freya pulled back her head and those gorgeous eyes of his awaited her.

Richard was not one to spoil the moment, but his conscience niggled and he wanted to make things absolutely clear to Freya. People could trust him with their lives, but not with their hearts, and he wanted to be sure she understood that before things went further.

'Don't rely on me.'

It was the oddest thing to say, perhaps, and yet the kindest.

'I get it, Richard.'

He wasn't going to be the cure for her loneliness. Richard Lewis wasn't going to be the love of her life.

Yesterday it might have mattered. But now she knew it didn't have to last for ever, or even for more than this night, because her time in London was finite. And she *wanted* this night with him.

It was Freya who moved to close the gap between their mouths. But it was definitely Richard who kissed her, softly at first, but warmly and thoroughly. Freya's mouth felt so exquisitely tender that even the gentlest of his kisses felt bruising.

The moan as his tongue slipped inside came from her. And then, for the first time since she'd arrived, London fell silent. Save for the sound of *them*.

His breathing was ragged and their mouths were frenzied. And surely he'd kissed the oxygen from her because he made her dizzy, and his tongue was so expert and thorough that it made her crave more of him.

His hands undid the belt of her robe. He freed one arm, then the other, and as it slid to the floor she felt cool air on the back of her body—a contrast to the warm rough fabric of his suit and the press of metal and buttons on her naked front.

Freya had never known such raw passion. Their tongues jostled and then she was pressing herself into him, her hands clutching his hair as his hands spanned her waist.

He guided them so that they moved to the wall as if as one. His kisses were certainly not smooth now—they were indecent and delicious and Freya was lost in them. Their chins bumped, their teeth clashed. She wanted to climb him and wrap her body around him.

Freya was tackling his belt, to free him, and then she felt his hard warmth leap towards her hand.

Richard reached into his jacket pocket for a condom, and it was an impatient pause for them both as he sheathed himself. She ached to have him inside her, and he ached to be there too.

And so he rectified things, thrusting in and taking her against the wall.

Freya had never been so thoroughly taken, and it felt sublime. He lifted her so that her legs could wrap around him and she knew she had never moved so seductively. He exposed a side to her that she did not recognise, because she had always been a touch reticent in bed.

Not now.

His fingers dug into her buttocks as she ground against him, and instead of feeling herself holding back, she was *more* herself with him.

She was so light that he could put one hand against the wall and hold her round her waist with the other. And then he changed the pace...

There was a scream building in her throat, which was clamped closed, so it waited there, trying to burst free. And then there came a breathless shout from him, followed by a rush of energy along her spine as he came deep within her. Finally her scream found its release, but it came out in staccato sobs as she throbbed to his beat.

His hands soothed now, rather than inflamed, and he seemed to know that this wasn't a Freya she knew.

And it wasn't.

Her head came to his shoulder and she felt the fabric of his jacket. He was completely dressed, and she was utterly naked. And now there was a smidgen of shame creeping in for Freya—just a curl of guilt as he lowered her down to the floor, yet still held her tightly.

He buried his head in her damp hair and then she felt his lips near her ear. 'I only wanted a cup of tea.'

Richard made her laugh. He just did.

Having sorted out his clothes, he picked up her robe and helped her into it, then did up the very same belt she had so readily allowed him to open.

They were both still a touch breathless, still trying to find their balance again,—but, *God*, they felt better.

She went and sat on the sofa, where she'd been lying earlier. Richard looked utterly normal—not even particularly dishevelled. His hair fell into perfect shape, whereas Freya was quite sure hers was in knots.

But she didn't care.

He came and joined her on the sofa, and though they didn't speak it wasn't awkward. It was nice to lie down with her head on his lap, looking up at him as he played with her hair. It was relaxing *not* to speak.

He looked around at her flat and saw for the first time the mustard carpet and odd curtains. Even odder, though, was the fact that there was nothing that spoke of *her*.

Well, there were some books and magazines on a shelf, but there was a large picture on the wall of a horse and carriage, and he was certain it hadn't been wrapped in a blanket and lovingly moved down from Scotland.

'Do you like horses, Freya?' he asked.

'Not particularly. Why?'

'There's a picture of one on your wall.'

She looked over to where his gaze fell. 'I know. I can't get it down.'

Well, that wasn't quite true. Freya had a little step ladder, which she'd used when she'd re-hung the curtains, but she simply hadn't got around to taking the horse and cart picture down. It wasn't as if she had anything to replace it with. It would do for now.

And, anyway, there were far better things to look at. Gosh, it was nice to lie there, Freya thought, looking up at Richard.

And for Richard it was nice too—nice to feel her hair, because it had entranced him.

He looked down, but not into her eyes. Her robe was hanging open a little, and he could see the curve of her breast and the edge of a pink areola beckoning. He wanted to slip his hand in...

But sustenance first.

'I'm starving.'

He wasn't asking her to cook for him—a bowl of cereal was his usual choice when in a rush, and he *was* in a rush. To resume proceedings!

He hauled her off his lap and walked through

to her tiny kitchen, where he opened up the cupboards while Freya lay there, liking it that he hadn't asked if he could do so.

Usually that would have made her tense. She recalled well how she had sucked in a breath when she had bought her little cottage and Malcolm had opened her fridge. But now she lay smiling as Richard opened and closed her cupboards.

'You have absolutely nothing to eat,' Richard said when he came back. 'Not even cereal.'

'I meant to stop at the shops on the way home from work. I think there's some soup...'

'That's not going to cut it. Come on,' he said. 'Get dressed.'

'We could always ring for pizza,' Freya suggested.

He was tempted. There was a huge appeal in the thought of having pizza delivered and then moving straight to bed. And he had seen from his search of the fridge that there was a bottle of wine there.

A perfect evening.

Except—rarely for him—the pleasure was laced with guilt.

Did she fully get that he didn't *do* the dating thing?

He wasn't that bad—it wasn't *all* bed. Just… mostly.

He had come here tonight fully intending to take Freya to that damned film—which was actually quite a concession for him. Richard couldn't remember the last time he had been to the cinema.

But now he had to be clear. Richard wanted to make sure that she didn't think this might lead to anything more than a few casual dates and a whole lot of bed.

While he hoped he had spelled things out yesterday—and although getting pizza and going straight to bed would be easier and far more pleasant—Richard knew that he needed to tell her that this night wouldn't change anything.

Yet clearly it was going to.

For they were soon back at the Italian restaurant—but as lovers this time.

CHAPTER SIX

TONIGHT IT WAS Richard who had the carbonara.

Freya chose spaghetti, and it came with a rich, meaty tomato sauce.

'You did it again,' Richard said.

'What?'

'When I saw your carbonara last night I regretted my choice…' And then he stopped, because he'd been about to say that next time they came here the spaghetti with the rich, meaty tomato sauce was what he'd want.

But he didn't.

Instead he remembered he was off work tomorrow and ordered a bottle of red.

'I don't like drinking if I'm working the next day,' he explained. 'But I've got a few days off now.'

'And me.' Freya smiled.

He wondered if she was waiting for him to suggest they do something together.

Ah yes, *The Talk*, Richard reminded himself.

Except Freya got there first.

'I'm going home for a couple of days before a stint on nights,' she said. 'I've got a new lot of tenants arriving at my cottage next week.'

'Holidaymakers?' Richard said.

'Yes, they're there for two weeks and then I've another lot coming in. I've arranged for someone to come in and clean, and change the sheets and things, but I just need to sort a few things out.'

'Don't you hate having people staying at your house?'

'I've put a lot of stuff in the cellar,' Freya said. 'And that's locked. It doesn't bother me.'

'But isn't it a hassle?'

'Not really.' Freya shrugged. 'And even if it is at times, then it's worth it. It helps a lot with the mortgage, though in a couple of months it's going on the market...' Freya halted.

Or was it?

She recalled that just before Richard had arrived her plans had started to change. She needed to be alone to think about that, to decide what she was going to do, and so she asked about him instead.

'What about you? Do you have plans?'

'I have an interview.'

'Ah, that explains the haircut,' Freya said as she twirled spaghetti around her fork.

'Not really. I was well overdue for that. It's not an interview as such—more an informal lunch to suss things out…'

He let out a sigh and promptly forgot the reason he had brought her here. Instead he told her what tomorrow was about. No-one else knew.

'There's a role coming up.'

'I thought you loved what you do?'

'And I do, but it *is* consuming. I'm actually heading to the airport after the lunch. I'm going to Moscow tomorrow for a few nights, to get away completely.'

'Moscow?'

'It's a bit drastic, I know, but I love getting away. I don't put my phone on, so the hospital can't call me to come in—or if they do I don't hear it.'

'Well, you don't need to go all the way to Moscow for that. There are more than a few places in Scotland where you can't get a signal.'

'Please…' He grinned. 'I was teasing about changing the movie reels.'

'I know you were,' Freya agreed. 'But, trust me, there really are plenty of places you can't get a signal. I went away for Christmas with my family last year and we all had to keep going for walks just so we could make a call, or check emails and things. And in summer, depending on what provider they have, the tourists often can't get a good signal. We have a wee laugh, watching them walking around with their phones in the air.'

'Well, I'll bear that in mind,' Richard said.

'So, are you keen for this job?'

'I'm curious, certainly.'

He told her the name of a very exclusive private hospital which made her look up from her pasta.

'I've a friend, Marcus, who's director of anaesthetics there, and there's a position coming up—a very attractive one…' He didn't get to finish, for Freya had a question.

'But won't you miss the adrenaline?'

'Yes,' he said. 'But there are days when I think

no, I won't miss it at all. It's a big decision—but you'd know all about that, given you've just made a big move yourself.'

Freya gave a shrug. 'I just knew that I wanted to get away.'

He looked at her through slightly narrowed, assessing eyes. 'Why?'

'Lots of reasons,' Freya said. 'I had a bit of a rough year. Well, not myself, exactly...' She didn't know why it was so hard simply to say it. 'My best friend lost a baby last year... Andrew.'

'Were you present at the birth?' Richard asked.

'Not at the actual birth, but I was there on admission.' Freya said. 'Alison ended up having a crash Caesarean. She came in a week before her due date, everything about the pregnancy had been fine, and then I went to check the foetal heart-rate...' She paused a moment as she recalled it. 'At first I thought I had picked up Alison's...'

She didn't, of course, need to explain to him that the mother's heart-rate was usually a lot slower than the baby's.

'But then I knew the heart-rate was the baby's...'

'Not good.'

'No.' She shook her head. 'My senior, Betty, was there, and a doctor was there within a minute, and everything was set in motion. We got her straight upstairs to Theatre. I didn't go in. Betty knew I was too involved. He was born flat and was resuscitated but died two days later. Cord compression and meconium aspiration...' Freya screwed her eyes closed for just a second but then opened them and gave an uncomfortable shrug. 'Anyway, it was a difficult time.'

'Did she blame you?'

'Oh, no—nothing like that. It was more...' Freya didn't know how to describe how she'd felt when she didn't really know herself.

'You blamed yourself?'

'A bit,' Freya said. 'Well, I questioned myself. It made me realise that being so involved with my patients isn't always ideal.'

'So you came to nice, anonymous London?'

'It wasn't just because of that,' Freya said, 'but it is nice to be not so involved with the patients.'

'I'm sorry—you don't get to do a job like yours and *not* get involved.'

'It's not that easy...'

'I never said anything about *easy*.'

That annoyed her. Richard was too brusque, too direct, and he had hit a nerve.

'You don't know me.'

'I'm trying to.'

It was a rare admission for him, because while he might be talking about getting involved professionally, he certainly did his best not to on the personal front.

'You cannot do this job, Freya, and not care. Or rather, you cannot do this job in the way you want to do it and not care.'

He signalled for the bill and then remembered that they still hadn't had *The Talk*.

It didn't seem so important now. Freya was off to Scotland tomorrow and he to Moscow. And she certainly wasn't jumping up and down demanding to know when they would see each other again as they headed to the Underground.

'You really don't have to see me home,' Freya said.

'I'm not,' Richard said. 'I believe in equality—it's your turn to see me to my door.'

CHAPTER SEVEN

UH-OH!

Freya woke to a very un-lumpy mattress—in fact, she felt as if she was wrapped in cotton wool. And then she heard Richard speaking into the phone.

Her one and only one-night stand was over.

And, instead of regretting it, she smiled as she lay there, recalling last night.

They had arrived back at his gorgeous apartment and he'd poured them a drink and headed off for a shower.

She'd ended up in there with him.

And then they'd taken their drinks to bed.

Oh, it had been bliss.

She lay there listening to his lovely deep voice.

'No, I'm away until Tuesday, so I can't,' he said. 'How is Mrs Eames?'

As soon as the call ended, his phone went again.

'No,' he said, very brusquely. 'You cannot come and stay.'

Freya wondered if it was an ex, trying to get her toes back past the bedroom door, but she blinked when he spoke again.

'Mother, I have a friend staying at the flat while I'm away.' Pause. 'I *do*. Currently she's living in a terrible rental and I've loaned her the place for a few days. So, no, you can't come and stay. If you need a break from your fiancé then I suggest that perhaps you actually speak to him about that fact, rather than go away.'

Another pause and Freya rolled over and looked at him, not even politely attempting to pretend she was asleep.

'What do you mean, you don't believe me?' he said. 'Freya, would you tell my mother that my place is yours for a few days?'

Gosh, what a way to meet the parents, Freya thought as he handed her his phone.

'Hello, Mrs…' Freya didn't know what to call her, given she had divorced Mr Lewis three husbands ago.

'Amanda,' the woman said for her. 'So you're staying at Richard's?'

'Just for a wee while,' Freya said. 'While my landlord's sorting…'

'Pardon?' his mother said.

Richard took back the phone.

'So you see there is no spare room at the inn. I'll talk to you when I'm back from Moscow.'

He ended the call and his phone rang yet again.

'Work,' he muttered, and Freya didn't blame him a bit when he turned it off.

'Thanks for that!' Freya said with an edge, more than a little annoyed to have been put in that position and at his jab about her home.

'I never said you were my lover,' he pointed out, 'just that my apartment wasn't free. Anyway, she can afford a hotel.'

'Fair enough.' Freya said, but she was still sulking a little.

'I am *so* tired of her dramas.'

Freya said nothing.

'Can you see why I've been put off relationships for life?'

'I think so.' Freya nodded. He was *almost* forgiven. 'How's Louise?' she asked.

'Mrs Eames?' he checked. 'She's made it through the night and is holding her own. She's a lot better than yesterday at least.' He looked over. 'Do you want some breakfast or are you still cross?'

'Still cross,' Freya said and told him why. 'My flat isn't terrible.'

'I just said that as an excuse to my mother. She's hardly going to drop in and see it.'

'I guess…'

She let it go, and she decided he was completely forgiven when he got out of bed and returned with coffee, and toast topped with grapefruit marmalade.

Or was it the fact that she simply had to know more about this man?

'Were she and your father ever happy?' Freya asked as they ate their breakfast and got crumbs in his gorgeous bed.

'I think so. But she wanted a livelier social life and he is rather wedded to his job. She gave him an ultimatum and it backfired, I fear, because he chose work.'

'Your father married again?'

'Yes—his housekeeper. Or rather the woman who had been *their* housekeeper, so you can imagine how well that went down. My mother was convinced there had been something going on all along...' He rolled his eyes and then, putting his plate down, moved to take her mug. 'Can we talk about *our* sex-life instead, please?'

'But your parents' sex-life is so much more interesting!'

'Then I must be losing my touch.'

They made each other laugh and then, to Freya's surprise, and seemingly to Richard's, instead of taking her mug he lay back on the pillows and told her some more.

'She walked out when I was fifteen—a couple of days after their twentieth wedding anniversary. My father wasn't giving her the attention she felt she deserved. He had a terminally ill patient and had had to cancel their anniversary trip. I felt terrible for my father after the break-up—he just moped around. Then, just when I was starting my "A" Levels, he announced he was marrying Vera.'

'The housekeeper?'

'Yes. And the following summer my mother married an old friend of my father's. A more glamorous version of him, really.'

'What happened to him?'

'She left him after five years, and after that I kind of tuned out. Now all I know is that she's engaged to Roger.'

'Have you met him?'

'Yes—a couple of dinners. He's a cosmetic dentist.' He pulled a face.

'What's wrong with being a cosmetic dentist?'

'Nothing. I just feel his eyes on my mouth every time we speak. I think he's trying to work out if I've got crowns. In *my* line of work we just ask!'

He looked over to Freya and gave her a very nice smile that showed stunningly even teeth.

'And *do* you have crowns?'

'Two—thanks to rugby.'

She looked right back at him, and as she did so she thought about him asking his patients about their dental work before he put them under. She looked into his eyes and Freya understood why patients so clearly trusted him.

Because *she* trusted him.

Of course she didn't know him very well yet, but that much she knew. And, Freya thought as they stared at each other, if she were terrified and scared for her life, or her baby's, his would be the eyes she would want to see.

No, she would never regret this. In the twelve hours since their lips had first met she had come alive to her body in a way she never had before.

She wanted to put down her mug and reach for his kiss. Or at the very least to ask him what day he'd get back from his trip, in the hope that she could see him. But then she recalled their rules, and peeled back the sheet rather than leaning in to his embrace.

'I'd better go. I have a train to catch.'

'What time?'

'Ten.'

'Then there's plenty of time.'

'No, I need to get back to mine to pack.'

'Fair enough,' Richard said.

He lay there with his hands behind his head as she dressed. He kept his mouth firmly closed.

It was deliberate, because a long weekend in Scotland with Freya sounded tempting—rather than flying to Moscow by himself and cramming in some sightseeing.

'Have a great trip,' Freya said.

'I will.' He put out his hand and she came and sat down on the bed.

'And good luck with your lunch,' she added.

'Thanks.'

It wasn't awkward when she left. More, it felt… *unfinished.*

Freya thought about him more than she ought as her train slid its way northwards.

It was packed, and there were no seats in the quiet carriage, so Freya put in her earbuds and tried to listen to music—but every song sounded as if it had been written about *them*. So she gave up with the music and chatted to the woman in the seat beside her.

She was a fellow Scot, so neither had to say *sorry*, or *I beg your pardon* once, and Freya found out from her that on weekends and public holidays you could sometimes get a cheap upgrade to First Class.

'I'll remember that,' Freya said, and then gazed out of the window and watched the rolling countryside. The clouds gathered and right on cue, as they crossed the border at Berwick-upon-Tweed, she saw grey skies and rain,

It made her smile.

The train travelled the rugged Scottish coastline, eating up the miles until they reached Edinburgh Castle. It was dark and powerful and towering over them, and her first glimpse of it in what felt like a long time caused Freya's heart to swell.

The train pulled into Waverley Station and it felt very good to be home. The station was busy as she checked the board for the next train to Cromayr Bay and saw that she had half an hour to kill.

Freya decided to buy some flowers for her little cottage, to brighten things up. As she was paying she could hear her phone beeping, and assumed it was Alison, or her mother, checking on what time her train would get in.

She nearly dropped the phone when she saw that it was Richard.

Lunch went well. I'll have my phone off for a few days now, but just wanted to say that I hope you have a nice break.

No kisses or fun little emojis. No clues to anything, really—but even getting a text was more than she had expected.

Freya hadn't expected anything. She'd hoped that she might see him again—of course she had—but this simple text… Well, it confused her. This didn't fit with how he had said it would be.

She honestly didn't know how to respond.

A part of her wanted to fire back smiley faces and pictures of tartan berets and Russian hats—just to keep it all light and breezy. Yet light and breezy wasn't how she felt when it came to Richard.

And so, when most women would be firing off a rapid response to a text from Richard Lewis, Freya—because she didn't know how to respond— instead sent the promised text to Alison, and then stuffed her phone back in her bag.

Freya had no intention of telling people about

Richard. Certainly she wouldn't be telling her parents. While Freya adored them, her mother Jean loved 'a wee natter', and—as Freya well knew—nothing stayed a secret in Cromayr Bay for very long.

Alison was a different matter. And she was there waiting when Freya got out at Cromayr Bay.

The clouds had parted and the sky was high and blue, and Alison was smiling widely as she waved to her.

'Look at you!' Freya smiled, because in the weeks that Freya had been away Alison had changed and was now sporting a lovely little bump.

'I know!' Her friend smiled back. 'Betty said that you can sometimes show a lot more quickly the second time around.'

Betty had clearly said easily what Freya hadn't been able to. And still Freya did not know why.

She had been dwelling on it for months now, and had even discussed it with Richard, but still she had a huge block when it came to speaking about the loss with her friend.

'I booked us a table at the Tavern for tonight,' Alison said as she drove her home.

'In the *restaurant*?' Freya checked, because usually they went for a curry, or just to the Tavern's bar. The restaurant was pricey, and rather grand, but she had heard right.

'Yes, it's closing for renovations next week. They're going to put a function room in at the top, and they're refurbishing the restaurant.'

Freya didn't like the sound of that—she loved it as it was.

'The bar's staying open, as well as the hotel, but I thought you might want to see the restaurant as it is one more time.'

Oh, she really did.

They took the hilly street approach and, rarely for summer, there was a parking spot close to Freya's cottage. They pulled in behind her little purple car.

'Do you want to come in?' Freya offered, but Alison shook her head.

'I've got to go and do a shop—I'll meet you in the Tavern bar at seven.'

'I'll see you there, then.'

'It's good to have you home, Freya.'

It was good to be here, Freya thought as she pushed open the door.

The drapes had been closed by Mrs Hunt after the last tenants, and Freya went around opening them up and letting in the late-afternoon sun. Then she turned on the hot water and caught up on her mail while she waited for it to warm.

And she did all she could not to think too much of Richard and what had happened last night.

She wouldn't be telling Alison. At least she didn't know whether or not to tell her.

Alison and Callum had been childhood sweethearts. And Freya wasn't sure her friend would understand.

Freya herself didn't understand.

She liked it that there was no risk of getting overly involved with Richard.

The break-up with Malcolm had been tricky. He'd kept messaging and coming round, turning up wherever she went, wanting to talk, to see if they could give it another go.

Well, she wouldn't be having that problem with Richard!

It was rather freeing.

* * *

It was nice to dress up and go out. She hadn't brought much with her, but she had a nice copper-coloured dress, and with heels it was dressy enough. Her hair was still rather wild from going to bed with it damp last night, so Freya wore it up and then added a dash of lipstick.

She glanced at her phone as she put the lipstick back in her bag, and then decided she'd do well to leave the phone at home, to prevent herself from replying to Richard.

She had no idea what she would say anyway.

Freya headed to the Tavern bar, and she felt herself tense a little as she walked inside. It was Friday night in Cromayr Bay, and that meant there was a fair chance Malcolm would be there. But thankfully there was no sign of him, and a moment or two later Alison arrived.

The Tavern really was gorgeous—a boutique hotel just off the main street, it was set high on a hill and offered a stunning version of Freya's favourite view of the Firth.

They climbed the steps to the restaurant and

were shown to their seats by a waitress. Then Gordon, the owner, came over.

'Are you two here for a last trip down memory lane?'

'Something like that.' Freya smiled.

'I remember you coming here when you passed your midwifery exams—och, and for your eighteenth too…'

'I'm going to miss the old place.' Alison sighed.

'Well, hopefully you'll love the new one just as much,' Gordon said, and then he talked them through the menu.

They made their choices—which was tough, because there was lobster brought in from the pots just that afternoon, and there was Dornoch lamb, as well as Freya's favourite, game pie. But she'd had that the last time she was here…

'I'm going to have the lamb, please,' Freya said.

'And I'll have the spelt and mushroom risotto,' Alison said.

Freya had wine, and Alison a mocktail, and they chatted about Freya's move to London.

'So, have you made any friends there yet?' Alison asked.

'Not really,' Freya admitted. 'They're very cliquey...' she started. Only that wasn't quite right. They were all very nice. 'I don't know what it is. I try, I just don't seem to fit in. Richard says I'm too subtle.'

'Richard?'

'A friend,' Freya said.

'So you *have* made one.'

'A temporary one.' Freya said. 'He's being interviewed for a plum new job in a private hospital.'

'In London?' Alison checked.

Freya nodded. 'And he'll get it—he's brilliant.'

'Well, if it's in London that doesn't have to stop you from being friends. So you *do* have one.'

'I guess...'

Alison smirked, because she knew Freya well, and from the little flush on her cheeks it was clear to her he was more than just a friend.

'It's just a temporary thing,' said Freya.

'Why?'

'Because temporary is all he does.'

'But that's not like you.' Alison frowned.

'Well, maybe it is. Look, we've been out a couple of times, and both of us know that it won't be going any further, and that actually suits me just fine.'

'Why?' Alison asked again.

'It just does,' Freya said, and gave an uncomfortable shrug.

She wasn't ready to tell Alison she was thinking of coming home for good once her contract was up, but thankfully then their meals arrived.

The lamb was delectable and the conversation became easier. Alison chatted about her and Callum's tenth wedding anniversary, which was soon coming up.

'Can you believe it?'

'Not really.' Freya laughed. 'It feels like just a couple of years ago that I was your bridesmaid.'

'Are you coming home for your thirtieth?' Alison asked.

'I think so,' Freya said. 'Though I'm doing all I can not to think about that.'

They had a wonderful night catching up. Although not about the things that hurt.

As Freya walked down the hill for home the air was salty, and despite the late hour the sky was still dusky. It was so much lighter here than in London. But autumn would soon close in.

It was one of the reasons she'd come home.

Tomorrow she had to speak to the estate agent about house prices and things, as soon the families renting for summer breaks would fade away and her little slice of potential heaven would be going on the market.

It would be a relief, Freya told herself. The rentals covered the mortgage, but there was a lot of work to be done on her home.

A lot.

She let herself in and smiled at the pretty flowers she'd set by the window. Then she made herself a hot chocolate, frothing the milk in her coffee machine, and took herself to bed.

Freya rarely closed the curtains. There was nothing between her little cottage and the water, and the sight of the bridges always had her in awe. They were miles away, of course, but it looked as if fairy lights had been expertly strung in the sky, and the new Queensferry Crossing was magnificent.

Tomorrow she was catching up with a few

friends, and then there was a huge Sunday dinner at her parents' house to look forward to.

And then she thought about Alison and what she'd said about 'temporary' not usually suiting her. Perhaps now it did.

She took out her phone and read again the text he had sent.

Freya liked Richard.

A lot.

From the moment she had first seen him he had captivated her.

Yet she wanted to keep things breezy and light.

Or rather, she *had* to.

And not just because Richard Lewis had told her that it was the only way they could be. It was also because this place was home. Not London.

Freya had made up her mind now—she would not be selling her home.

He'd noticed her lack of response to his text.

Of course he had.

Richard had been moving through Security at Heathrow when he'd fired it off, and had regretted the simple message the second after he'd hit 'send'.

He did not report in to *anyone*—certainly not about things like interviews—and, furthermore, he loathed the cascade of texts that all too often came when he was seeing someone.

When he'd collected his phone on the other side of Security he'd seen that she hadn't responded.

Good, he'd told himself. A mistake had been made, but a lesson had been learnt, he'd decided as he had boarded the plane.

'Phones to be turned off now, please,' the steward said, but Richard had checked his again before he did so.

Four hours later, as he stood at Moscow airport, even though the very reason for his trip was to get away from the constant buzz of pagers and phones, he found himself turning it on.

No, she had not replied.

Freya could not have known the effect on him.

It made him want her more.

And that did not sit well with Richard.

CHAPTER EIGHT

'How was Moscow?'

This time it was Freya who put her tray down at his table in the canteen. It was morning—just after seven—and he was eating cereal.

Unlike her, though, he was starting his day rather than at the tail-end of a shift.

They hadn't really spoken since she had got back. Freya was just finishing a two-week stint on nights and their rosters hadn't crossed.

'Beautiful,' Richard said. 'But far from relaxing. All the signs are in Russian.'

'I wonder why!'

'Still, it was nice to get away. How was Scotland?'

'I had a great time. It flew by, though.'

'Have you finished on nights?' He frowned, because it was odd to see her down here at this time of the morning.

'Officially I have.' Freya nodded. 'But there's a twin pregnancy to deliver soon.'

Freya was lacking in experience there, as the birthing centre at home didn't accept multiple pregnancies. So she was more than happy to stay back—especially as through the night she had got to know Jeanette and her partner.

'Stella just came on, and she suggested I go and get something to eat. Then she and Dr Mina are going to hold my hand, so to speak.'

Neither mentioned catching up with each other again. Some things were best left, Richard had decided.

He liked her a lot—perhaps because he couldn't quite read her. She was private, and he liked that. And her eyes could be sullen at times, but then she punched out a smile...

All Richard knew was that he liked her a whole lot more than he was comfortable with.

'Your interview went well?' Freya checked, alluding to the text she hadn't responded to.

'It was just lunch.'

He offered no more, for he had already told her more than he should. Yet deep down he knew she wouldn't have told anyone his potential news. He'd never have shared it with her otherwise.

Richard hadn't expected to be as impressed as he was by the private hospital set-up. The hours were far fewer, though he could take on more if he chose, and he would have considerably more annual leave.

'It would be a step up—a big one.'

'A step back too,' Freya said. 'From the pace here.'

It wasn't a criticism. She looked at him and could see his exhaustion, and then she looked down at the pile of cereal with which he fuelled his day.

She looked up again, at the closed look on his face, and knew she should not have come over. It wasn't just their rosters that had kept them apart. He was politely avoiding her.

Thankfully, this time around it was her pager that interrupted them. 'Woohoo!' Freya said as she glanced down and read the message it was time for her to go back up to Maternity. 'Wish me luck.'

She didn't wait around to hear him do so. Instead, she made her speedy way along the yellow line to Maternity and pushed the gorgeous Richard Lewis out of her mind.

Having washed her hands, she headed into D4.

'You've been busy,' Freya said to Jeanette as she tied on a plastic gown. 'Well done, you.'

The next hour was sheer hard work for Jeanette and she did it brilliantly. Freya made sure there was no trace of tiredness in her own reactions.

The room started to fill up. Guy Masters and his registrar came—one for each baby—as well as Stella and Kelly.

'Listen to Freya,' Dr Mina said as Jeanette started to panic.

'You're almost there,' Freya encouraged. 'A big one now...'

She had never delivered twins before, but with so much experience in the room she didn't feel at all scared. And as Twin One was delivered onto Jeanette's stomach there was a sense of elation.

Yet there was more work still to do.

'Is she okay?' Jeanette kept asking over her baby's cries.

'She's wonderful,' Kelly said. 'Dad, do you want to cut the cord?'

With Twin One in Kelly's extremely capable hands Freya prepared to deliver Twin Two. The baby was in a good position, and Freya looked up and saw that Jeanette was starting to push.

'Well done,' Freya said. 'Jeanette, you are doing *so* well...' Being a midwife was such a privilege, she thought. 'Okay, I need another big push.'

And then Twin Two was there, a little stunned and straight off to Stella, and soon there was the delicious sound of two babies crying.

'Well done,' Dr Mina said quietly to Freya.

'Thank you.'

There was still the single placenta to come, and when it did both Freya and Dr Mina carefully examined it and checked the membranes.

Soon the room was clear. The paediatric team were happy, and Stella and Kelly had dashed off. Everything was under control here.

They were utterly adorable, Freya thought as she helped Jeanette feed her twins one by one. Once Jeanette was on the ward and wasn't feeling so shaky she would be helped to feed them both at the same time, but for now they lay in their mother's arms one at a time.

'You were completely wonderful.' Freya smiled.

'So were you,' said Jeanette.

Freya was feeling a little shaky herself after her first twin birth. She wrote up her notes and filled in all the paperwork, but the words blurred a little on the page.

Because of tears.

She was tired, that was all, Freya told herself as she pressed her fingers into her eyes. She was tired and over-emotional. And now that the birth was over she could take her thoughts back to the canteen, and to the ending of her and Richard.

Oh, but she'd been warned. Not just by Stella but by the man himself.

'Home?' Stella gently asked.

'Yes.'

Freya stood and made her way to the changing rooms. And suddenly, coming down from the L&D theatre, there he was.

'How did it go?'

'It was brilliant.' She smiled deliberately.

'Have a well-earned sleep, now.'

'Thanks.'

And that was it, Freya thought as she closed the

door. They were back to niceties on passing in the corridor and no more.

She peeled off her baggy top as she started to change so she could finally go home. But then came a knock on the door.

'Freya...?'

She lifted her top to cover herself, and then didn't know why she needed to bother, given it was him.

He wanted to apologise—to tell her the problem was him, not her—but they didn't get there.

Richard never brought any personal awkwardness to work. He had his pickings, but he never allowed things to get awkward *here*.

Yet suddenly they were kissing.

Deep, frantic kisses.

She found out that his rough unshaven jaw was possibly her preference over the clean-shaven version. And then he was thumbing her nipples through her bra.

'Not here...' he said, even as he pressed into her.

He had moved from her mouth and was kissing her neck, and his hand was creeping into the back of her navy trousers.

The scent of him was potent and she found his mouth again and…

Oh, God, she was nearly coming.

'Not here,' he said again, and sort of shoved her off him.

It was probably just as well, or they'd have been on the floor of the changing room, where anybody could walk in.

They both breathed through it and waited for it pass, but it was a couple of minutes before Richard was ready to head back out there.

'I'll text you about tonight,' Richard said.

Freya noted that he didn't sound happy or flirty or teasing. He sounded frustrated. As if it was *her* fault for the situation they were in, when it had been Richard who had followed her in here.

'And answer my text this time, Freya.'

CHAPTER NINE

BOTH OF THEM kept waiting for the bubble to burst.

Yet it didn't.

They tended to end up at his place, but one morning two months into *them*, and three months after Freya had moved to London, Freya stirred on her lumpy bed with Richard spooned in behind her.

It should be over with by now, she knew. Freya was waiting for Richard to discard her with the practised ease he was known for.

And, oh, it would hurt.

It would hurt like hell.

London would be lonely without him. Friends had proved very hard to come by, and the pace of the work still completely floored her. She missed being more involved with the mothers, and found she craved the community that had felt too small.

Freya was homesick.

For home, for family and friends.

Apart from during her time with Richard—which was wonderful, of course—Freya ached for home.

She was starting to do what he'd told her not to.

She was starting to rely on him.

And while Freya waited to be summarily dumped, Richard waited, as Freya had once said, for the very curl of her hair to irk him.

For the gloss to fade.

For the joy to wear off.

But it hadn't. It didn't.

If anything, it had intensified.

He lifted her hair and in the darkness could see her pale skin. He pushed down the sheet.

It was a cold mid-October morning and she shivered, both from the chill of the air and also the heat as he ran a finger down her spine.

And then he brought his tongue to her neck.

He slipped a hand under her so he could play with her breast, and she groaned as he toyed with her nipple.

'Wake up,' he whispered.

'I don't want to,' Freya whispered back. 'I'm having a lovely dream.'

She could feel him hard against her thighs, so she parted them a little and he slipped between their warmth.

He really should reach for a condom. But this was so nice…

He probed between her thighs, teasing, rubbing, caressing the edges of her intimate space without pushing in.

Freya knew she should halt things. Yes, she was on the Pill, but that wasn't the point. They had made no promises to each other—just sex for as long as they both wanted it.

But then there were the dinners and the breakfasts. and the talking into the small hours at times.

Though there was little talking now…

But, ever the sensible playboy, he did not slip into her inviting warmth. He pulled away from between her thighs and Freya lay with her eyes screwed closed in frustration as he sheathed himself.

She was losing her head—Freya knew that. And she dared not check her heart.

He came back to his previous position and groaned, '*God*, Freya,' as he slipped in.

She was so ready and tight, and pre-dawn sex had never felt better. He filled her and stretched her, and his body wrapped around hers felt like a blissful vice. He toyed with her breast in the way she had come to adore.

They moved in delicious unison, their bodies tuned to each other, pressing together until they found their climax.

They lay on their backs on her lumpy mattress, both sated and breathless, but when the near-miss with the condom came to her mind Freya gave him a scolding.

'We have to be more careful.'

But he hadn't *wanted* to be careful, and, Richard knew, neither had she.

'We'll talk about it.'

'No,' Freya said, 'we already have.'

She was not sleeping with someone who had told her never to rely on him without a condom.

And yet Richard was starting to rely on her in a way he had never considered he might.

Life felt a whole lot better with Freya in it.

Yes, work was crazy, but there was a counterbalance to it now, and he needed far fewer trips overseas to get away from the pressure.

Instead, he looked forward to the end of a workday and to nights spent with her.

He didn't like coming *here* so much, mind… He didn't like her poky flat. But last night he hadn't finished until midnight, and he had hardly been able to ask her to hop on the Tube and come to his place. Or give her a key and tell her to come to his at the end of her shift and let herself in.

Surely it was way too soon for that? And, anyway, he'd sworn never to get so involved.

Yet more and more he found he was.

It was Richard who broke the silence. 'Marcus is pushing me for an answer on the new job.'

'And have you decided what you want to do?

'Not yet. It would mean starting in the New Year.'

'That's ages away.'

'It will be November in a couple of weeks,' he pointed out. 'And I'd have to give a month's notice—more if possible. So if I want some time off between jobs then I need to give him an answer soon.'

'Which way are you leaning?'

'I'm still not sure,' Richard admitted. 'The private work would be at a slower pace, and seriously more money...'

'But you *love* what you do.'

'I know that, but...' He ground down on his jaw.

He wanted her take on things, but whenever he broached it with Freya she asked only what *he* wanted to do. And, while he liked it that Freya never put any kind of pressure on him, he kind of needed her view on this.

Because it might affect her.

God, he thought. He was staring up at the ceiling and wanting someone else's input into his future because he was starting to think, to *hope*, that the 'someone else' might be involved in it.

He thought it better not to say anything just yet, though. He really needed to think this through, and he needed to get the hell out of here before he went and said something stupid.

He had always been incredibly focused where work was concerned, and independent in his choices too. This way of thinking was a huge shift for him, and lying in the warmth of her bed it would be all too easy to offer her his keys, to move her in, because he did not want her here in this horrible flat.

He wanted her at his home.

'I'm going to go,' Richard said.

'There's still an hour before you have to leave.'

'Yes, but I want to have a shower...'

'Have one here.' Freya frowned.

'I don't like your shower, Freya,' Richard said, and climbed from the bed.

Ooh, what was that all about? Freya pondered as Richard dressed. He was in an odd mood, and as he went to leave he gave her only a brief kiss on the cheek—more like a family member might at a gathering, rather than a lover who had just left her bed.

Freya could not let it go. 'Thanks, Uncle Richard.'

'What?' He frowned.

'That's the sort of kiss my uncle gives me,' she said, and looked at him with accusing eyes.

He smiled, because he couldn't help but smile

when she was around, and because she was such a snarky thing that he was tempted to dress her, pack a case and haul her back to his place.

For good.

'We'll talk tonight,' Richard said. 'You're on a late?'

'Yes.'

'Well, I finish at six, but I'll stay back and then we can go to mine.'

He walked out of her flat and Freya heard the slam of the door. She lay there, not quite so brave now.

Richard wanted to talk.

To Freya that could only spell one thing.

They were done.

She had known the winds would change eventually, and that one day he'd tire and Rita the domestic would be reaching under a bed with a broom for her soon to be discarded heart.

She had been duly warned.

Freya had sworn to herself that when the time came she would be ready for it and fully prepared to deal with it. Except she hadn't factored in how deeply feelings could be etched. Never had she felt such kinship with someone. And as she got up and pulled back the curtains a world without Richard in it suddenly looked a lot less friendly than even a cold grey day in London.

She showered and told herself she was over-reacting. Of *course* Richard wanted to go home to shower—because hers was horrible, with dark green tiles, and the water ran cold for ages before you could get in. And the shower curtain needed to be replaced.

She had meant to get another one, but she was always running out of time in between work and Richard. Still, after her shift today she had two days off. She would get on with sorting out the flat then.

God, imagine being here without him, Freya thought as she sat on the Underground and looked at the endless faces that refused to acknowledge her and the eyes that flicked away the second the mistake of eye contact was made.

It was another busy late shift, and close to the end of it she turned at the sound of her name.

'Freya. There's a phone call for you. Private.'

'Oh.'

Very deliberately, Freya had left her mobile in her locker. The only people she could think of who might call her at work were her parents.

Tentatively she picked up the phone. 'Freya Ross speaking...'

'Freya?'

If ever the sound of your own name could drench you in ice, it did then to Freya. There was a begging tone in the voice that sounded like a final grab for a rescue rope.

It wasn't her mother, it was Alison, and Freya knew only too well the inflection of her friend's voice when it was laced with fear.

'I didn't want you to find out from anyone else,' Alison said, 'but Aunt Shona's already put something on social media and I'd rather you heard it from me...'

'What's happening?'

'I've had a bleed,' Alison said. 'I'm having tests, and Dr Campbell says that I might I have an abrupt—' She stumbled over the word.

'An abruption.'

This might well be serious and Freya felt sick.

And angry.

And scared.

But she held in her fears as Alison spoke again.

'They're not sure where the bleeding is coming from, but apparently I have an irritable uterus and they're monitoring how the baby is faring.'

'Are they looking to deliver?' Freya asked, and knew her voice had that odd, distant note she saved for Alison these days.

'Not at this stage,' Alison said, 'but they're monitoring me, and might transfer me from Cromayr to Edinburgh, if needed. Freya, I'm so scared.'

'I know you are, but sometimes bleeds happen. It doesn't necessarily mean—'

'Freya!' Alison interrupted. 'Can you come?'

Her request was unexpected. Welcome, yet unexpected. They were best friends, and yet somehow Freya had felt Alison might want her to stay away this time.

'Of course I'll come,' Freya said. 'I've a couple of hours to go on this shift and then I'm off for a couple of days. I'll turn my phone on now and you can call me if anything changes. If you're transferred, tell Callum to let me know and I'll come straight in to see you at Edinburgh. I'll be there in the morning.'

'Is everything okay, Freya?' Stella asked as she hung up the phone.

'No,' she admitted. 'My best friend's pregnant and she's had a bleed and has been admitted. She lost a baby last year, so I'm going to head home at the end of my shift. I'll take the train.'

'Do you need me to take a look at the off-duty?'

'I should be fine. I've got a couple of days off.'

'Well, the night staff will be arriving soon, and there's enough of us on if you want to go.'

As their conversation was ending Richard arrived at the desk. He dealt with some questions that Stella had for him, and then the first chance he could Richard spoke to Freya. 'I shouldn't be too much longer,' he said. 'If I run a little over can you wait in the staff room?'

Oh, right, Freya thought. Their talk. He wanted to speak to her, and Freya was quite sure that it was about the end of them.

'I can't come over tonight,' she told him. 'Alison's had a bleed and she's asked me to go and see her. Stella's letting me go early, so I'm just about to go home and pack and then I'm heading to Euston.'

'How bad is it?' Richard asked.

'It sounds as if it's under control,' Freya said. 'And if there are any further issues then she'll be transferred to Edinburgh. I think she's just terrified…'

'And needs a friend?'

'I guess… Or maybe she doesn't understand what's happening and wants me to translate what's been said.'

'I'm quite sure they've told her exactly what's happening,' Richard said. 'If you can give me half an hour to sort out some cover, I'll drive you.'

Freya shook a head. 'It's fine. I'll just go home and pack a few bits—the Tube's just as quick.'

'I meant that I'll drive you up to Scotland.'

She'd thought he'd meant he would drive her to Euston.

'Sorry?' She frowned, unsure if she was hearing things right. 'Don't be daft. You're back on in the morning, and you're first on call.' Freya knew his roster as well as her own. 'We wouldn't even get there until then.'

'It's not daft at all,' Richard said. 'I'll sort it out. Just give me some time to arrange cover.'

'You don't have to do that.'

'Freya, in the same way I'd do it for them, my colleagues will cover for me when it's urgent.'

He could not know how much those words meant to her.

'You're sure?' Freya checked.

'Of course I am.'

This was unlike anything Freya was used to. *She* was the fixer. The one who sorted things. Even as she had hung up the phone on Alison she had already been mentally working out the off-duty roster and the train times to Edinburgh.

And yet here was Richard, calling on colleagues and rearranging his schedule.

Stella was marvellous too and, unasked, swapped around her next set of days off, so that she had four days off in a row.

'Though if Kelly is swapping her weekend with you, then I'll need you back for an early on Monday.'

Freya nodded. 'That would be great,' she said. 'Thank you so much.'

She had a quick shower in the staff changing rooms, and by the time she came out Richard was ready.

'All done.'

Richard made it sound like a simple feat had been achieved. He didn't burden her with the drama of it, he simply sorted it, and within the half-hour they were driving towards her flat.

There wasn't a hope of him getting a parking spot, but he said he'd drive around while she packed.

'Wait on the pavement for me.' Richard said.

He drove around and in the end he did find a spot, beside a small café. He ordered two coffees and four pastries and then headed back to her street. She was waiting for him, dressed in jeans and a long baggy jumper with an overnight bag beside her.

Richard negotiated the car through the traffic and filled her in with what he'd achieved while she'd been in her flat.

'I booked myself a room at the Tavern.'

'Why?' Freya frowned.

'Well, given your cottage is being rented out, I

didn't want you to have to go to the bother of explaining me to your parents.'

'No,' Freya said, 'the last tenants are gone.'

'Oh, that's right—it's on the market.'

Except it wasn't on the market. Because Freya had decided against it, given that she knew she was coming back once her London contract was finished.

But she couldn't deal with telling him that tonight, Freya thought. She would save it for when she was summarily dumped.

Yet it didn't *feel* like the end of them, Freya thought, still more than a touch stunned that Richard had changed his busy schedule just to make things easier on her.

'The satnav estimates that we'll be there at seven,' Richard told her. 'Maybe call when we get closer and check that she hasn't been transferred?'

'I will.' Freya nodded. 'I'll pop in and see her when I get there, if she's still in Cromayr Bay, though I might have to wait until visiting hours if she's been transferred to Edinburgh.'

'We'll know soon enough,' Richard said.

They chatted idly for the first couple of hours, but then she decided to be brave and address what he had said this morning. 'You said that you wanted to talk to me?'

'It's nothing that can't keep.'

'We have five hours to go,' Freya pointed out.

But Richard shook his head. 'It's nothing that can't keep,' he said again.

Perhaps he didn't want a hysterical crying female in the car as he drove, Freya pondered, although she was determined to at least *pretend* to take it well.

She looked over to him and her heart skipped, as it always did. Yes, she'd sworn to take it well—it was what they had agreed on after all. But she would miss him so.

Richard turned the conversation to his work, and she could not know, just how rare that was—because usually he didn't discuss such things in depth with someone he was seeing.

Generally it was just a case of replying, 'Busy day,' to any enquiries about work.

Not tonight, though.

'I just signed off on Dominic performing epidurals,' Richard said. 'That's going to make things a lot easier.'

'That's good.'

'He's brilliant,' Richard mused.

'Have you told *him* that?' Freya both smiled and yawned as she asked the question.

'Not yet.' He glanced over. 'Why don't you try and get some sleep?' he suggested. 'I'll wake you when we stop for petrol.'

'Okay, then I can drive when you get tired.'

'I'll be fine.'

Freya rested her head against the window and very soon was drifting off.

Occasionally she stirred, but there was just the radio playing and the lulling sound of a car eating up the miles.

When she finally woke she glanced at her phone.

'Anything?'

'No.'

'Well, no news is good news,' Richard said. 'We're coming up for the border—we'll stop after that.'

And there it was, the blue and white flag of Scotland as they crossed the border, and it felt both odd and nice to be doing it with Richard. It was good to be home.

The motorway stop was efficient.

She went and bought them something to eat while he filled up the car. 'Why don't you get flowers here for your friend?' he suggested.

Freya bought a gorgeous orchid, and a bunch of flowers for herself, and soon they were back in the car for the last leg. They were just merging onto the motorway when he let out a curse.

'What?' Freya said, looking around, assuming a car had cut them up or was driving too closely behind them.

'I forgot to get condoms.'

Freya was shocked, because she'd been expecting to be dumped but then she smiled. 'We do have shops in Cromayr Bay.'

'I know. But I've never run out of supplies or not had any to hand...'

'Never?'

'God, no. I wouldn't leave it to someone else. There would be little Richards everywhere...' He gave a shudder at the very thought.

'I'm the same,' Freya said.

She didn't leave that type of thing to anyone else either, and kept right on taking her Pill regardless.

The hills were dotted with wind turbines, but rather than soothe her as they drew closer to their destination Freya found she was nervous.

'I don't know what to say to her,' Freya admitted as they neared the stunning Queensferry Crossing. 'I was so hoping that what happened last time was just a one-off.'

He glanced over. 'She's had a bleed—it could just be a scare,' he pointed out. 'Did the same thing happen last time?'

'No…' Freya shook her head and then sighed. 'It's not just the baby I'm worried about. Things have been a bit strained between us. I don't know how to *be* with her.'

'Just be yourself.'

Freya let out a laugh that was so close to tears it was almost a sob. 'I don't think she needs my anxiety right now. I'll just keep things calm and point out that this type of thing…' She halted, because when she had tried to say that to Alison on the phone, Alison had suddenly cut in and asked her to come.

'Can you stop being a midwife?' Richard asked.

'I'm trying to. We're really close, but I just don't know how to be around her lately. I keep saying the wrong thing, or not saying what I know I should. It's ironic, really, when I've been taught, and I'm well-versed on how to deal with grieving mothers.'

'Well, you can be trained to the back teeth, but it's very different when it's a private grief. No one *always* knows what to say,' Richard said. 'You try, of course, and then you find out that it wasn't the right thing at the right time, or it was the right thing but at the wrong time.'

He was speaking about himself, Freya realised. 'Did you lose someone?'

Richard nodded. 'Marcus—the guy I'm considering working with—his son died a few years ago. He came in at nine in the evening with meningococcal and was dead by sunrise the next day.'

'Were you working at the time?'

'No.'

He looked over again and saw the slight dismissal in her eyes that told him he couldn't understand what she'd been through. Richard had stayed quiet on the subject before, because that was when he had still been determined to keep things light between them. When Freya had still just been his way of getting away from things for a while.

He wasn't trying to get away from things now, and so he spoke on. 'For a long time I wished to God that I *had* been working.'

She looked at him. 'You don't mean that.'

'But I do,' Richard said. 'For close to a year, nearly every day I wished that I'd been on call that night and been the one dealing with him.'

He thought back to that time, and to the hopelessness and anger he had felt.

'I convinced myself that had I been on then I'd have picked things up sooner. In my God-like moments—' he gave a black smile '—the moments when I'm able to control the world, I decided that had I been there I could have changed the outcome. But in the end I worked out that no matter how much I wanted things to have been different, there are some outcomes that can't be changed.'

'No...' She had never really thought of it like that.

'Just stop for a moment and imagine that you hadn't been on that night.'

'I can't,' Freya said. 'I still have nightmares about it.'

'I know you do,' Richard admitted.

He'd never mentioned it, but he had felt her panic sometimes as he'd held her through the night. She would sit up for a moment, and then eventually settle back to sleep. It had felt like a private thing—something she perhaps didn't want him to have seen—and so he had left it. Because they weren't supposed to have the kind of relationship where you noticed things like that.

But he wasn't leaving things unsaid now.

'Suppose you were a teacher, or you worked in a shop, or even on one of the other wards and you hadn't been there that night...'

'But I *was* there.'

'Just stop,' he said again. 'Just take yourself out

of the picture. Suppose you hadn't been on duty that night—how would you have felt?'

'I can't take myself out of the picture, Richard. I was *there*.'

They stopped talking about it then, because some sights were just too beautiful not to pause and take them in.

The dark sky had turned to grey, with soft blushes of pink starting to emerge, but now, as they approached the crossing, they were bathed in gold and pink and it felt as if they were driving through fire.

'That's stunning,' Richard commented.

'I know,' Freya said. 'I never tire of it. I can see the bridges from my bedroom. It's a sight to behold.'

She rang and found out that Alison hadn't been transferred and they arrived in Cromayr Bay along with the morning. Freya directed him along an easier route than the satnav recommended, and soon they were pulling into the parking area near the ambulance bay.

'I'll try not to be too long,' she said.

'Take your time,' Richard said. 'I'll be asleep.'

It was nice not to be running up the corridor harried after two train journeys and weighed down with an overnight bag. Instead Freya had on lipstick and was carrying a huge orchid as she made her way up the corridor. And, no, she did not need a red arrow to find her way.

Laura, the Matron, greeted her warmly. 'Things are looking better,' she said as Freya approached, putting her at ease straight away. 'We were going to transfer her last night, in case the baby needed to be delivered. It's still an option, of course, but everything has settled down and Dr Campbell thinks for now she can stay here. Any further bleeding, though, and she'll be off to somewhere with a NICU.'

Freya let out a breath of relief as Laura took her through.

'She's going to be so pleased to see you.'

And Alison was.

Sitting up in bed, strapped to a CTG monitor, she was having a cup of tea. She put it straight down and then promptly burst into tears when she saw her friend.

'It's fine,' Freya said, and gave her a cuddle.

She could hear the rapid bleep of the baby's heart and it was just the sweetest sound in the world. Especially now, today, here with her friend.

'I am so sorry to drag you up here. Especially now that things seem fine. But when they mentioned delivering me I just panicked.'

'Of course you did.' Freya said. 'But it sounds like things have settled down?'

Alison nodded.

'These things happen,' Freya said. 'It doesn't mean it's related to what happened with Andrew and that it's going to happen again.'

'So everyone keeps telling me—and the sensible part of me knows that,'

'But you're not thinking with your head?'

'No.'

They spoke for a good hour, but still Freya felt more midwife than friend—though by the time she was heading off Alison seemed a lot calmer.

'How long are you staying?'

'For a few days,' Freya said. 'They let me swap my off-duty, but I need to leave on Sunday. I'll come back at visiting time.'

'Did you come by train?'

'No.' Freya shook her head. 'A friend drove me.'

'Which friend?' Alison asked, with a look in her eye that Freya couldn't ignore.

'A good one.' Freya answered. 'And that's all I'm saying on the subject. I'll be back this afternoon.'

And that 'good friend' hadn't slept the hour away.

Richard had tried to, but he had found himself watching the distinct lack of emergencies at the casualty department at Cromayr Bay Hospital.

Oh, there was *some* activity—there were staff arriving for their shifts and some leaving—but not a single ambulance had pulled up.

One patient had arrived—a car had come into the forecourt and an elderly gentleman had spoken to a porter, who seemed also to man the doors. The porter had gone off and returned a few moments later with a wheelchair.

Richard had watched as they'd both helped a woman out of the front seat of the car. She'd been holding her wrist in a familiar way.

'Colles' fracture,' Richard had diagnosed from a distance.

God, he'd go out of his mind with boredom here.

And it was cold. So much colder than mid-October in London that he'd sat with the heating on in the car.

And now he saw Freya, smiling and walking. She stopped and chatted to the same porter, who must also be on duty for wheelchairs and things.

She was happy here. Richard could see that.

'Hey.' He gave her a smile as she climbed into the warmth of the car. 'How is she?'

'Better than it sounded last night. If she has another bleed they'll transfer her, though things are calm for now. I'll go in and see her again later today.'

'Sounds good.'

'It does.' Freya nodded. 'I can't thank you enough for this. It all seems like a bit of a false alarm now.'

'Well, thank God it was.'

'Did you cancel the room at the Tavern?'

'No,' Richard said. 'I thought that so long as your friend's okay we might both go there for dinner tonight. It sounds amazing.'

'The restaurant's new,' Freya said as she directed him the short distance to her home. 'I really want to see it. I hope they still do their game pie. It's the best you'll ever have tasted.'

'It will be the *first* I've ever tasted,' Richard admitted, and then he gave her thigh a squeeze. 'And maybe we can slip upstairs to my room after.'

'I think I like the sound of that.' Freya smiled—and then brought them down to earth with a bump. 'I need milk.'

'I need sleep.'

They pulled in at a small store, but after a moment, rather than wait in the car, Richard, knowing the emptiness of her shelves in London, got out to make sure that she got things like bread and eggs too.

Yes, he was hungry.

And, no, he would not be buying condoms, Richard decided.

Another thing to add to the discussion list tonight.

Romantic dinners in Scotland, discussing his work and then sex minus a condom—he'd be asking her to move in next.

The oddest thing of all was that the thought didn't terrify him…

He held open the door for a woman who was wheeling a pram and saw that Freya was standing behind a large gentleman, waiting to pay for her milk.

'Did you get bread?' he asked patiently.

'No.'

'Do you have butter?'

'No.'

'Is there anything else you need?' Richard checked.

'I don't believe so.'

'Anything else *at all*?'

He meant for tonight, and they both knew it.

And when he looked at her like that, when he smiled, she forgot her fears. She forgot the temporary nature of *them*.

'Nothing I can think of.' Freya smiled.

As he headed off to get bread and butter, and nothing else, he heard someone call her name.

'Freya!'

She turned and gave a huge smile. 'Mrs Roberts!'

'It's Leah,' she reminded her, and Richard watched as Freya peered into the pram.

'Oh, she's beautiful!'

The baby really was. A gorgeous smiling baby, who was wide awake and looking up at her. There were certain babies that just had to be held.

'Do you mind?' Freya checked.

Leah laughed 'Go ahead.'

Richard was back, so she handed him the milk to hold as she unstrapped the baby.

'Oh, my...' Freya said. 'She is absolutely *gorgeous.*'

'She really is,' said Mrs Roberts, and then she glanced to Richard.

Freya remembered her manners. 'This is Richard Lewis—he's a friend of mine from London.'

'It's lovely to meet you, Richard. I'm Leah Roberts. I went through a bit of a time and...well, Freya really helped.'

'I'm glad to hear it,' Richard said. 'What have you called your daughter?'

'Freya,' Mrs Roberts said, and then looked to Freya. 'And, no, it wasn't just because I like the name—though of course I do. You really helped me. You were so kind through my pregnancy. I kept wanting to talk to you, though I didn't know how to.'

'You did it in the end,' Freya pointed out.

'Yes—Norma came down to help, and I had Mrs Hunt come in for the first few weeks...' She looked at her daughter. 'I got to actually *enjoy* her. And though of course I didn't care if it was a boy or a girl, she was a wonderful surprise.' As Freya handed her back, Leah gazed fondly upon her daughter. 'She's a true blessing.'

'Everything went well with the labour?' Freya checked.

'It did. Betty was wonderful, of course, but I did miss you so.'

He drove the last few minutes to her home, with Freya directing him.

'Mine's the blue one—though we'll have to park a bit further up. It can be hard when there are lots of visitors.'

Richard parked, and as he climbed out the scent of the sea reached him. The sun was glistening on the water and there was an angry seagull squawking above as they walked down to her cottage.

Richard had to stoop to get in.

Her home was cold from being empty, and Mrs Hunt had closed the curtains. And yet it was gorgeous, Richard thought as they stepped in and she pulled back the lounge curtains and let in some light.

'I'll put the heating on,' Freya said. 'It's a bit early to light a fire.'

Freya ran a vase under the tap and put the flowers on the table, in the hope of brightening it up.

'Do you want a coffee?' she called out.

'No, all I want right now is bed.'

He was beat. A long day at work and a very long drive up to Scotland meant all he wanted to do was stretch out.

'I'll just have a shower first.'

'You'll have to wait for the water to warm—it will take half an hour or so.'

After turning on the tank in the airing cupboard she showed him the tiny bathroom, and then took him through to her bedroom. The curtains were already drawn closed, and as he stepped into the soft darkness of her room and saw the large bed, the thought of waiting half an hour for hot water held no appeal. So Richard started to undress.

'Are you coming to bed?' he asked.

'Not yet,' Freya said, because unlike Richard she had slept in the car. 'I should maybe let my family know I'm here, and then I might go and…' Her voice trailed off.

Because that was what looking at him did to her at times. Freya needed no reminders as to his beauty. All she ever had to do was turn her head. But here in the dark bedroom, with the lights off, it was not that which swayed her—more the thought of Richard in *her* bed, and the waste of a morning spent on the phone, taking care of a hundred little jobs, when she could be with him.

'I might just join you.'

He was already in. 'God, your bed's comfortable.'

'I know,' Freya agreed. 'I found this mattress topper…'

She was speaking to a less than captivated audience. The bear was asleep. In her bed.

Bears could be many things. Intimidating, irresistible… She stood there, mulling it over, but couldn't think of another adjective. She just knew that she wanted to lie with him, her bear, in her bed.

Freya set the alarm on her phone, so that she'd be up for visiting time, and undressed. She had forgotten how cold her house could get. Or maybe the goosebumps could be labelled as a sign of tiredness.

Either way, she was cold as she slipped into bed, and then she was colder still from the chill of neglected sheets against her skin.

But then Richard rolled over and wrapped her in his arms and she no longer felt cold.

She slept warm in his embrace, and struggled to wake to the sound of an alarm that was pinging somewhere, reminding Freya of where she needed to be.

She rolled onto her back and her brain scrambled to orientate.

She was home…

Alison. Visiting hours. Get up. Get dressed. Be there.

Except she was here.

Feeling his hot mouth on her breast and the sensual slow suck that had made a place low in her stomach draw tight.

It was as if he knew, for his fingers traced slow circles there, and then crept down, down, all the way down…

And then he left her breast, and as his mouth found hers his fingers worked magic.

She moaned, and he liked it. She should really reach for him, but she was feeling too selfish to move.

The alarm went off again, but neither of them cared. She was locked in the bliss of a kiss that delivered ten thousand volts and a hand that did the same.

Her hand went to the back of his head and he swallowed her throaty gasps. Freya could hear the sound of her sex, slick and wet, as he brought her to the boil. He kissed her while she came, and when he rolled atop her it didn't feel disorientating, more like the right place to be on this earth.

As he slid, unsheathed, inside her, her whole body shivered with desire.

It had never been better for either of them. The tight and yet slippery grip of her...the absolute union of them.

He moved, but it was slowly, and he savoured the feel of each thrust and the slow draw-out followed by the faster pushing in.

She was digging her fingers into his back in an effort to hold on to her thoughts and reel them in. Because they were making love, Freya knew. They were *making love*.

They had done many things, but never this.

They were kissing and then pausing to look at each other. And she was in a heated frenzy of passion and emotion as he took her deeply, because a part of her wanted him to pause, while the other part wanted him never to stop.

He took her harder now, and she forgot to hold on. Her thoughts simply unravelled until there was nothing left in her mind but the shattering of *them*. As he shuddered he spilled himself deep inside her and she throbbed against him. The bliss of her clenching made Richard moan, and those last precious drops came to the fading twitches of her climax.

And as he lay there, spent and still inside her, Freya opened her eyes and stared at the ceiling as she found the word she had been missing before.

Irreplaceable.

There would never be another who came close to him.

Richard Lewis was irreplaceable in her heart.

And that shook her to her core.

This wasn't some fling. It might have started as such, but now it couldn't end without regrets.

Not any more.

Freya knew that when it ended he would be leaving with her heart, and she must not let that show.

And so she wriggled out from under him and then climbed from the bed. 'I have to go and visit Alison.'

She really did have to go, or she'd be late for visiting time. But she knew her voice was distant, cold, detached.

'I'll just have a quick shower,' Richard said, pulling back the sheet.

But Freya stopped him. 'You don't need to get up—my car's outside.'

That surprised him. Richard didn't really know why. He'd just assumed that the little purple car blocking his way belonged to a tourist—a visitor or a neighbour. It had never entered his head that it was hers.

'My dad drives it to work once a week,' Freya explained as she headed for the shower. 'To keep the battery from dying.'

Richard dozed as Freya showered, and then she came back in, wearing the same grey dress she'd had on the day they had met. Now, though, underneath it, she had on a long-sleeved black top, as well as thick black tights. Her hair was up, and he saw she'd added a little lipstick as she came and sat on the bed.

'I'll be a couple of hours.'

'Take your time.'

'There's everything you need in the kitchen. Well, there's coffee, and your bread and things, but I'll bring us back a fish supper. They do the best here.'

'And there was me thinking you were finally going to cook.'

They parted with a smile and he heard her footsteps leave and then the sound of the door closing behind her.

Her father needed to drive her car rather more frequently than he currently was, Richard thought as he lay there, because it was taking her a few goes to get the engine ticking over.

Richard was fully awake.

Automatically he checked his phone, and then checked and checked again. But, as Freya had once predicted, he had no signal.

The seagull which had been calling for the last half-hour had found a friend or two, and they were all being rather vocal, yet it wasn't that keeping him from going back to sleep.

'To keep the battery from dying.'

Louder than the seagulls, Richard replayed Freya's words, frowning as he mulled over them. They felt important, and yet he told himself it had just been a throwaway phrase.

He gave up on sleep and headed through the lounge and into her tiny kitchen, taking a moment to work out her rather fancy coffee machine.

As he got the milk out Richard read a note on the fridge, presumably for holidaymakers, reminding them to turn the water off at night and explaining a few nuances of the place.

He walked through to the lounge, and while, yes, it needed a helluva lot of work, it really was gorgeous.

There were books on the shelves, and little ornaments and shells dotted around. As well as that there were paintings on the wall that *she* had put there—not prints of some ugly old horse and cart. And there were throw rugs on the sofa.

'To keep the battery from dying.'

Now he understood why he had stalled on those words.

This was Freya's home.

And she was keeping it going as it awaited her return.

Richard walked through to the bedroom and opened the drapes and let in the view.

It was stunning.

Afternoon had given way to dusk and the lights from the bridge had come on. Richard found himself wondering what it must look like deep in winter.

He made another coffee and lay there, looking

out but not enjoying it as he had on first sight. For he really knew her some more now.

'Two fish suppers, please.' Freya smiled as she placed her order. 'And a large tub of the home-made tartar sauce.'

'It's good to see you back, Freya. Are you here to see Alison?'

Of course the world already knew.

'Aye, I've just been in to see her—she's looking well.'

It was just the kind of normal idle chatter that happened in this place all the time, Freya thought, and she realised she had missed it.

'Will you be wanting pickled onions?'

She was about to say no, even though she loved them, but perhaps they would both be eating them, Freya thought with a smile. 'Two, please.'

As she drove up the hill to the cottage Freya felt her spirits buoyed. Their lovemaking had been blissful, and Alison had been looking brighter. And now she was simply enjoying the familiar rhythm of home.

Made all the better because Richard was here.

Yes, her mood was good.

It was a lot darker here than in London, and the clocks changing in a couple of weeks would make it darker still. But, unlike many, Freya loved winter and embraced its grey approach.

She'd said before that it was a bit early to be lighting a fire, Freya thought as she parked on her street, but there was a cold chill in the air as she got out. A fire would make the cottage so very cosy.

And, Freya thought as she turned the key in the door, it would be nice to sit by the fire with him.

The house was in darkness. She guessed that Richard must still be sleeping, so she put the supper down and got out plates, then found glasses for wine.

And to hell with it.

She lit a fire.

'Richard?' Freya pushed open her bedroom door. 'Supper's…'

Her voice trailed off as she saw that he was awake and sitting up in bed.

'Enjoying the view?' Freya asked as she looked out fondly to where his gaze fell.

'Not particularly.'

She frowned at the unexpected response and looked out to the bridges. Such had been his tone that she had almost expected them somehow to have changed. For a fire to have broken out on one of them. Or some drama to be unfolding with flashing lights.

But the change was in him, in the room.

'You never really moved to London, did you?'

She frowned at his question, and at the slightly hoarse note in his usually smooth voice.

'I don't know what you mean.'

'I mean,' he snapped, 'that you've never really left here.'

'Of course I have.'

'Is the house up for sale?'

'Not yet.'

'Freya, why didn't you bring your coffee machine down to London?'

It was the oddest question, and she frowned as she gave a simple answer. 'Because I couldn't fit it in my dad's car.'

'And you bought flowers without thinking about it for this place, to pretty it up, yet your flat in London barely gets a look.'

'Richard, I've been busy, and most of my time off is spent at yours.'

'Oh, come off it, Freya,' he snapped again.

Since the moment she'd left to visit Alison he'd been giving it some considerable thought. And all his thoughts pointed to the same conclusion.

'Is this why you've no real interest in whether I take the private job or carry on at the Primary?'

Freya swallowed.

And Richard saw her swallow and knew he was right.

God! He had been going to ask her to move in with him—to take things further! He had even gone to Freya for her take on his career in case it affected *them*.

Well, he decided, she never needed to know that.

'It's been your intention to come back here all along.'

'No,' Freya argued. '*No*. Richard, when I left I thought it was for good. I truly did. I was so tired

of this place, and everywhere I went there were...'
She didn't know how to explain it. 'Reminders.'

'Of Malcolm?'

He hoped not. God, he seriously hoped not. But
he *had* to rule that one out.

He saw her eyes screw up and the tiny, impatient, shake of her head as she completely discounted that. He believed that it had had nothing
to do with the other man.

'The baby?' Richard checked, and her silence
was his answer. 'You left because you were upset
about your friend's baby?'

He didn't say it scornfully. She saved the scorn
for herself.

'Not just the baby. Alison too. I know it shouldn't
get to me the way it does. Even Alison seems so
much better, and I guess I appear so too. I should
have got over it—I know that...'

'Freya, you're grieving.'

'No.' That sounded too dramatic a word. 'Maybe
at first, but it was Alison who lost—'

He spoke over her. 'There aren't numbered tickets given out for grieving. You don't get sent to the back of the queue just because the baby wasn't yours. You went through a bad time at work and the loss was a very personal one. Then you ended a long-term relationship.'

'I was right to.'

'Yes, but it might have been more than you could deal with at the time so you ran away.'

'No.'

But Richard wouldn't let her off that lightly. 'Did you know Alison was trying for another baby?'

'Yes.'

'You couldn't face it if anything went wrong and so you left, but you were always going to come home.'

Had she been?

Freya thought of her last days in Cromayr Bay and the ache in her heart as she had walked out of the delivery centre for the last time.

Not the last time *ever*.

A part of her had known that even then.

Even if she had brushed it from her mind.

'Yes.' She admitted it now. 'But I didn't know that when I applied to work at the Primary. I didn't even know it for certain when I started seeing you.'

'But you do now?'

Freya nodded.

And, for the first time in his life knew that the biter had been bitten.

'Richard, you and I...'

'We were a fling.' He let out a mirthless laugh.

She had meant them to be just that, Freya knew. It had never been going anywhere, or so she had thought, and so she had been able to close her heart and have fun for once. But it had been a grown-up game she'd been playing, which meant when it went wrong there was a greater risk of hurt.

He climbed out of bed—and it was odd the things you noticed, she thought, but he turned away from her to get dressed, when he had never come close to doing so before. A glimpse of that beautiful body was denied to her.

'Do you know what *really* annoys me?' Richard's voice was as brusque as the hands that tucked in his shirt.

'That I wasn't honest with you? I accept that, but I truly didn't know how I felt—'

'No,' Richard interrupted. 'The part that *really* annoys me is that you never gave London a chance.'

'I did.'

'No, you had it pegged from the start as cold and unfriendly.'

Given the circumstances, Richard figured he deserved a chance to be mean, and he used it well.

'I'll tell you why you've got no friends, Freya. It's because—unlike me—people probably sensed that you were never really serious about being there.'

'I take my job very seriously.'

'I'm not questioning your midwifery skills. I'm saying that you never gave London a chance.' He shook his head. 'I'm going.'

'Where?'

'To the Tavern. I hear they do a nice game pie.'

'Don't go,' Freya implored. 'We can talk. Surely?'

'And say what? Is it your intention to come back and live here?'

There was no point dressing it up, so Freya told him the decision she had made. 'I'm going to see my contract out and then I'm moving back here. It doesn't mean we have to stop seeing each other. Lots of long-distance relationships work out…'

His laugh was almost a shout. Every word sounded foreign to him.

Long. Distance. Relationship.

A few months ago it might have been ideal. He had been growing tired of casual relationships. With Freya in Scotland he could still focus on work…

God, they were so bloody good together that if he stayed—if they ended this row in bed—he could actually see himself saying that he might consider moving here.

But his decision as to what to do was already complicated enough. He did not need another iron in the fire. He was not, *not*, going to consider living here.

Never.

'Enjoy the view, Freya.'

He didn't need to slam the door, for the bitter tone to his voice reverberated through her far more than the sound of wood on wood could.

Her one-night stand had proved to be more.
And yet he had gone without working through it.
Gone without hearing her side.
Gone.

CHAPTER TEN

FIRST CLASS.

It felt incongruent to Freya that she should lug her broken heart back to London in style, but she'd learnt a few tricks, having made the journey so often, and, given it was Sunday and there was a spare seat, she'd got a cheap upgrade.

Freya wasn't just lugging her heart home, though.

She had thought hard about what Richard had said about her never having given London a chance, and she had spoken about it to Alison too, when she'd visited.

'I'm torn,' Freya had admitted. 'If I stay it will only be because of him. And what happens when he decides it's not working out? He won't even talk to me about it. No.' She'd shaken her head. '*This* is home.'

'Well, why don't you try and make *London* home for a while?' Alison had suggested.

'That's where I'm headed tomorrow.' Freya had given her friend's stomach a tender caress. 'If this wee one behaves.'

Between visits to her friend Freya had braved the cellar of her home and filled up some cases.

The coffee machine would have to wait. It was simply too heavy. But she had packed some rugs and photos and ornaments, and now she sat on the train with her luggage stowed as a tall woman pushed the buffet cart to the side of her table.

An elderly lady stirred nearby and gave Freya a smile as she selected a Ploughman's sandwich and a bag of crisps and then promptly fell back to sleep.

Freya was grateful for the silent carriage, for there was only the lulling movement of the train and the stunning countryside to take the edge off the frequent barbs of her thoughts.

Richard's words had stung so much because they were true. Freya hadn't set out to hurt him, yet inadvertently she had.

And so she looked at her phone, which was on silent, and this time there was no thought of Russian emojis or tartan berets.

This time her text was from the heart.

I never thought I would feel the way I do about you.

While he sat in his gorgeous apartment, surrounded by tiny pieces of Freya—a silk scarf over his sofa, a pair of earrings on his table—knowing that there was some of her washing in the tumble dryer, he read her second text.

Does it have to be all or nothing?

Her question was both sensible and ridiculous.
Sensible because they'd been seeing each other for just a couple of months, and it was too early in the piece to be speaking of career and country moves. Ridiculous because they both knew how they felt.
Richard texted back.

Can you see yourself staying in London?

Freya answered.

I don't know.

* * *

Freya had answered, but sensed that now wasn't the time to lie.

She looked out of the window as the train slowed down and they arrived at Berwick-upon-Tweed. She recalled being in his car as they crossed the border. The feeling of being home.

And then, as they left Berwick-upon-Tweed behind, she felt torn from the land of her heart. No, she could not see herself permanently in London.

Not really.

And so she sent another text.

No.

Silence was his first response. But as the train pulled into Newcastle her phone pinged.

There's no point, then.

He was as brusque as ever.

Richard, we can't do this by text. I'm on the train now. Can I come over?

* * *

He read the message and gave a wry smile, for all too often a lover had pleaded with him via this very vehicle not to end things, and asked could they please just come over and talk.

This felt like a very different message from the familiar.

It would end in bed, rather than tears, Richard knew, and they would be no further along than they were now.

No, you can't come over. I'll meet you at Euston.

Richard wasn't on the platform, but as she came through the barrier and stepped out into brighter skies her heart sank. He looked amazing, in black jeans and a thin black jumper, but when she saw her own bag over his shoulder Freya knew that the things she'd left at his flat were inside.

'I'm sorry I wasn't honest with you,' Freya said. 'That first night we went out I'd only just started to figure out that I wasn't planning on staying after the end of my contract.'

'Pardon?'

She looked into his gorgeous eyes and managed a pale smile, because she knew he was teasing, as well as trying to ease the pain and make their parting of ways as good as it could be.

'I kept waiting for you to dump me,' Freya said, and poked at his lovely big chest. '*That's* what it said on the box. I went into this with eyes wide open, knowing we had a fast-approaching use-by date...'

'I know you did.' His sigh was a weary one, and it came from lack of sleep—though for once that had nothing to do with work, for he had been on days off.

'Nothing has to change...' Freya attempted, but even she could hear the futility behind her words, because so much already had.

He handed her the bag. 'I don't want us to see each other any more.'

'Richard, please,' Freya said, even when she had sworn she would never beg him not to leave. 'Don't rush off.'

He had to.

Lest he stayed.

'You don't have to make a decision now,' Freya reasoned as she ran after him.

'I've already made it,' Richard said.

'I can't believe you won't let us talk.'

Infuriatingly, he shrugged.

She spoke on. 'I've still got a couple of months to go here, and *some* long-distance relationships work...'

He didn't want to hear it. Richard did not want this dragged out. He did not want his precious days off spent on the motorway, and he did not want her the best part of a day away. So, rather than admit to the hurt he felt, instead he was blunt.

'I like sex a bit more regularly than once a fortnight.'

Her mouth clamped closed. She really didn't have an answer to that.

But Richard hadn't finished yet.

'You wanted a bastard you could readily leave behind, Freya,' he reminded her. 'Don't complain when I deliver.'

And, as she had been promised by all and sundry, as she had known would happen on the day she had accepted a night out in his company, Richard Lewis broke her heart.

'Don't!' Freya warned the flower seller at the Underground station, before he could tell her again to cheer up because it might never happen.

But then she relented.

It had already happened.

She had lost Richard.

And the worst thing about that was that in everything he'd said he'd been right.

So she bought a huge bunch flowers, even though she didn't really feel like it, and lugged her cases up to her flat.

As she opened the door Freya winced.

Really! Imagine her bringing Richard back *here*.

The carpet was vile, but she had ordered a huge rug online that would soon be here, and she had brought loads of things from home.

Loads.

Okay, she only had three more months left here, but she was *not* going to just sit it out.

So she threw some gorgeous quilts over the sofa

and scattered cushions on top, and then she set to work putting out ornaments and pictures.

It was better that than focussing on a seriously broken heart.

At work, he ignored her.

Not in front of the patients, of course. And Richard was far too smooth to do something silly like call her 'Nurse'. He still called her Freya if he had to—just not quite in the same way he had said it before.

A couple of weeks into her heartache he came to the nurses' station, where Freya and Stella were sitting. He was wearing scrubs, and still had on a paper theatre hat.

Stella was sorting out the off-duty rota and Freya was feeding a very fussy Baby Glover, whose mother had been taken to Theatre post-delivery when complications had set in.

'How's Mrs Glover?' Stella asked.

'She's fine.' Richard nodded. 'And she should be back on the ward soon.'

He didn't look over or say hi to Freya. He just sat and caught up with the notes he'd been writing before he'd had to dash off. Mid-stroke of his pen, though, he peeled off his cap and tossed it into the bin.

The cap had left his hair messy, just as it had been on the day they had met.

Now Freya knew why.

'Felicity,' Stella said. 'I mean Freya—can you swap from an early to a late on Tuesday?'

'That's fine.'

Freya no longer took it personally when Stella got her staff's names muddled up, because when it came to babies and mother's names she never did.

Never. Not once.

And with twenty-eight mothers and babies on the maternity unit this morning alone, Stella had a lot on her mind.

'You don't have plans?' Stella checked.

'No,' Freya said. 'Well, actually I'm trying to make some curtains, but I'm sure they won't care if I don't get to them that night.'

'You should speak to Pat,' Stella said, but didn't elaborate, and then, having finished sorting out the off duty, she got up and walked off.

There wasn't silence.

That would be too much to ask mid-morning on a maternity ward.

But there was silence between *them*.

How she missed him.

'Richard?' Freya said, and looked up from the little infant she was feeding, 'Do you think—?'

'Is this about a patient?'

'No.'

'Work?'

'No.'

'Then you don't get to know my thoughts.' He stood. 'Dominic and my SHO are stuck in ICU, so I'm going down to Surgical to do the Pain Round. Tell Stella I'll be back to finish these notes when I get a chance.'

'Sure.'

He walked off.

Richard didn't *stalk* off—he didn't do anything other than put her neatly in her place.

He did the Pain Round and asked the patients over and over, 'On a scale of one to ten—ten being the highest—how would you rate your pain?'

'Ten,' some would say, while reaching for their cup of tea.

'Three,' some would say, just a few hours post-op, while wincing from the pull of stitches on their wound or the weight of a sheet.

And that night, when he went home to an apartment minus any little pieces of Freya, Richard dared not rate his own pain.

He had returned to London after their row to the sanity of a single life. It was now two weeks post-Freya and the pain should have improved considerably. In fact the old Richard would have been well onto the next woman by now. At the very least he should be out with a friend and mocking the fact that he had almost considered giving up all this for a career in Cromayr Bay.

Mocking it.

Laughing at the fact that in the days after they had ended things he had placed a call to the head of anaesthetics at Cromayr Bay and made tentative enquiries.

He had been invited for an informal visit in a couple of weeks, to be shown around. There were currently no vacancies, but he'd set the ball rolling. Richard knew he should halt it now.

He wasn't hungry enough to order take-away, so he ate cereal and then took off his suit and stepped into his pristine glass shower. But the trouble with that was he missed those awful green tiles at Freya's place, and the inevitable search for a towel.

Here he had his choice from eight white fluffy ones, all folded and waiting. Yet for all its luxurious bliss, his apartment felt as sterile as an operating theatre now that Freya wasn't there.

He lay in his non-lumpy bed and, though he might appear comfortable to some, he decided to rate his pain.

One to ten…with ten being the highest.

Seven? he attempted, because although it had hurt seeing her today he had been effective in cutting her off.

And yet he'd badly wanted to hear what she'd had to say.

Eight? Because he still hadn't cancelled his visit to Cromayr Bay, simply because he missed her so much.

Nine? Because he was a stubborn bastard and where his career was concerned he never backed down.

This damn thing called love hurt more than he'd considered it might.

Yes, love. And he missed her.

Ten.

Yes. Losing Freya was definitely a ten.

CHAPTER ELEVEN

As STELLA HAD SUGGESTED Freya had spoken to Pat—who, it turned out, was a fantastic seamstress.

'I'll do them for you,' Pat offered.

'I can't just bring you in a pile of fabric!'

'Don't be daft. I'll bring my sewing machine to you.'

It had been arranged for Sunday afternoon, and Kelly had come along, Stella too. As nervous as for a first date—in fact far more nervous than she had ever been on a date—Freya had bought cheese and nuts and crisps and worried.

But then they'd arrived, and it had been so much fun. Pat on the sewing machine, Stella on the ladder. And by the time they had left there had been deep crimson curtains.

They changed the entire room.

And he would never see them, Freya thought.

'Do you see him at all?' Alison asked one night when she called.

'A bit,' Freya said. 'Well, quite a lot. But it's not like before. His registrar, Dominic, can do most of the epidurals now, so I only really see him if there's an emergency.'

'Have you tried talking to him?'

'There's no point,' Freya said. 'He's made things completely clear. I don't see why I should have to give up coming home when he won't consider moving.'

There was silence. From both of them.

'I want you here,' Alison said finally. 'You know I do. But if Callum had to move for work—well, that's where I'd go.'

'Yes, but the fact is *you're* not working. You've finished work to have a baby,' Freya snapped, and then realised what she'd said. 'Sorry...'

'No!' Alison laughed. 'I'm delighted to hear the return of the real Freya. You've been...'

'What?'

'Too *nice*,' Alison said. 'Too *midwifey*.'

'I shall have to snap at you some more, then. Anyway, enough about me—how are *you* doing?'

Alison was doing well. The baby was due early in the New Year and Freya's contract was up in mid-January—which meant that Freya wouldn't be around for the birth.

Alison was having the baby in the main hospital, and if there were any further bleeds she would be transferred elsewhere, so there would have been no chance of Freya delivering her friend anyway.

Yet still she would have *been* there.

She thought back to the time when she had first put in her application to London. She and Malcolm had long since broken up, and Alison had just told her that she and Callum were expecting again.

They'd sat in the bar at the Tavern and Alison had said she wanted Freya to be with her in the delivery room.

'Callum's going to be so tense,' she'd explained.

'That might not be possible,' Freya had said, and had told her best friend that she was considering moving to London.

It had just tumbled from her lips, even before it had been a cohesive thought, and it had grown from there. Freya had applied for a job at the Primary the next week.

Richard had been right. She'd been running away.

There was no avoiding heartbreak, though. It just morphed into something else and found you wherever you were hiding.

Until you faced it.

CHAPTER TWELVE

RICHARD NO LONGER crashed out in the staff room, and they merely nodded if they met in the canteen.

Freya ached to know whether he had decided to stay with the NHS or go and work at the private hospital. Each week when the hospital newsletter came out Freya scanned it for information, but there was no mention of his leaving, nor of his replacement.

She'd find out on the intranet, perhaps. Or one day she would realise he was no longer here, Freya thought as she sat on the labour and delivery unit, where she'd been allocated today.

'It's so quiet,' Freya commented to Stella, for there was only the sound of a woman loudly humming her way through her contractions.

Pat was in there with her. And Kelly was in D5.

'Why don't you go and have your coffee break while it is?' said Stella.

'Freya,' Kelly called, because they were 'buddies' today. 'Can you check this CTG with me before you go?'

Freya did so. They both checked it carefully. There were a couple of anomalies—enough that they called over Stella, who then buzzed for Dr Mina to come and asses mother and baby.

'Go and have your coffee now,' Stella said.

Freya made a coffee and thought how odd it was that it would be a normal day in Cromayr Bay while she was here in London. They'd have the antenatal and postnatal clinics running through the day. And then there were care-in-the-home visits.

Freya loved those. Going into a home and seeing the new baby and its family. If there was a part of her job in Cromayr Bay that she missed the most, then it was that—following the entire journey.

Of course she followed up on certain cases here.

Louise Eames was doing incredibly well and had been discharged home. She was recovering from her trauma and visiting her tiny son.

But it didn't feel the same. Freya missed her old

work, the longer preparation and anticipation of birth and the follow up too.

She was about to open a magazine when the overhead chimes went off.

Freya didn't rinse her mug. Instead she put it down on the coffee table and headed straight back to a department that was no longer quiet.

The light was flashing over D5, and Stella was running for the phone. Then she saw Freya.

'Let Theatre know we've got a crash Caesarean coming,' she told Freya, and then got back into D5.

Freya made the call and saw Richard running down the corridor and into the same suite.

'Freya?' Stella put her head out through the door. 'Can you check this?'

As Freya went over to check on the drugs she could hear a tense conversation taking place between the father of the baby and Richard.

'But I'm her husband—absolutely I'm going into Theatre with her.'

'He won't get in the way,' the patient pleaded.

She was lying on her side, with oxygen, and Freya could hear the sound of the baby's heart-rate. It was ominously low. Her waters were thick with meconium, which was usually the baby's first bowel movement after birth.

It felt like a replay of what had happened to Alison.

Andrew had died from meconium aspiration.

Of course it happened—Freya knew that—but she could hear the fear in this mother's voice and it sounded just like Alison's had…

'What's happening?' she asked.

Her calls did not go unanswered as Stella, Dr Mina and Kelly all took time to explain as they prepared her for urgent transfer.

'Baby doesn't like the contractions,' said Dr Mina. 'The slow heart-rate tells us that.'

Then Stella spoke. 'And the meconium shows us that baby's distressed…'

Guy Masters arrived then, and got the handover from Dr Mina.

'I want Abigail in theatre,' Dr Mina said, and looked over to Stella. 'Now, or we go ahead here.'

'They're preparing.' Richard said, a touch breathless.

No one would move from this room until a theatre was ready, even if it meant that the baby was delivered here.

'I want my husband with me,' Abigail said.

And then Freya found out what Richard Lewis could accomplish in seconds.

'I understand that you want your husband to be there for the birth, Abigail,' he said in his deep voice. 'But you're having general anaesthetic so it just isn't possible. We need to get your baby out quickly.'

'I *insist* on being there!' the husband cut in.

'Mr Dunstan,' Richard said. 'We don't have time to debate. You *cannot* be there. From this point, I won't be leaving your wife's side.' He crouched down to be at eye level with Abigail. 'I will be with you the whole time until you are brought round.'

He didn't make false promises and say he'd be there after that, because he knew she would be handed over to the post-anaesthetic care unit, and at that point he might well be called to something else. He had just told the terrified parents how it would be, and had obviously reassured them at the same time, because Abigail nodded.

'Now,' he said as he stood, 'I've got another IV line in and I've gone through your history. I just need to ask if you have any dental crowns.'

'None.'

'Or any loose teeth that I should know about?'

'No.' Abigail shivered.

Everything was ready to go, and the emergency packs were ready for the short dash to Theatre, but until they were told it was ready they would not be leaving.

'Theatre's ready!' someone called.

And then they were off. Running down the corridor in a race to save the baby.

'Can you clear up?' Stella asked, when she saw Freya simply standing there in the middle of D5.

'Of course.'

She cleared all the discarded wrappings and equipment, and as she replaced the oxygen masks and tubing could see that her hands were shaking.

And then she stopped.

Just for a moment.

It felt as if she was shrouded in black lace.

Freya simply stood there and felt the fear and the absolute horror of that night with Alison. And then she did what Richard had suggested on the day that had ended them.

Her mind was in a time that had never been. Imagining a phone call and hearing that Alison had had the baby and it hadn't gone well. Or coming into work and hearing the news. Or Callum, Alison's husband, calling her.

'How would you have felt?' Richard had asked her.

Now Freya felt that moment without herself in the picture.

Devastated.

Only Richard wasn't there to know her answer.

Richard knew this patient would have upset Freya. It had been an incredibly close call.

Their aim was thirty minutes from alert to delivery, and in this instance it had been twenty-eight.

There could not be a more valuable two minutes saved, Richard thought now as he heard the cries of his patient's new baby and Abigail Dunstan was wheeled through to the post-anaesthetic unit. She had been extubated in Theatre and would soon come round.

Richard went over and spoke to Kelly. 'How is he?'

'Lucky,' Kelly said. 'He's well enough for a quick cuddle with Mum when she comes round, and then we're taking him up to NICU—but really just to be observed.'

'Good.' Richard said. 'Well done.'

'And you.'

It had been a good day. Or rather, a good hour. But at any given second that could all change.

Richard looked around at the efficient unit that he'd frequented so often and knew he was going to miss this place.

He was going to go private.

His decision was made.

Rather than hover, he headed straight from Theatre back to the Maternity Unit.

Yes, he should stay away from Freya, Richard knew that, but he was certain this case would have upset her.

He would check up on *any* staff member, Richard told himself. But he knew that he was lying, for every day involved drama after drama. If he checked in on everyone he'd never get anything done.

'Hey,' he said to Stella. 'Well done back there.'

'I heard he's doing well. What can I do for you, Richard?'

'I was actually looking for Freya.'

He didn't dress it up, or pretend he was here for another reason.

'She's gone home.'

'Oh.'

'A migraine, apparently.'

'I see…'

'She's back on tomorrow—on a late,' Stella said. 'And that reminds me… It's her birthday tomorrow. Can you sign the card?'

'I haven't got time for that. I need to get down to Surgical.'

'It will take two seconds!'

They did it for everyone. Just a cake and a card. It was nice that a staff birthday didn't escape unnoticed.

And so he took out his pen and scribbled a message.

Best wishes
Richard Lewis

Richard wrote what he always wrote—but he didn't feel like he always felt.

He needed time to think—but when did an anaesthetist in a busy hospital get that?

By the end of the day the good outcome with Baby Dunstan had been countered by the loss of a twenty-year-old, and as he drove home Richard changed his mind—no, he would *not* miss the place.

And the drama didn't end at work.

As the garage door beneath his apartment opened he was just pondering calling Freya, to check how she was faring, when he caught a flash of blonde hair. And as he got out of his car she rushed over to him and promptly burst into noisy tears.

Oh, God, Richard thought. *Not now. Please!*

CHAPTER THIRTEEN

THIRTY!

How the hell had *that* happened?

Freya awoke in a far less lumpy bed, thanks to the amazing mattress topper she had bought, and commenced her fourth decade on earth.

Whether she looked older or not, Freya thought as she came out of the bathroom and looked in the mirror, she didn't *feel* older—and she didn't feel wiser.

Freya just missed him so.

She was working a late shift, so she took her coffee back to bed and lay checking her messages. There were plenty, but Alison must have been waiting for her to switch on because her phone rang straight away.

'You're catching up to me,' Alison said.

'Ha-ha.'

'Thirty! It's awful, isn't it?'

'Not really. I feel the same as I did when I went to bed. It's just the numbers that have changed.'

'There's a parcel here for you,' Alison said. 'I'm not going to lie and pretend I've posted it. You're not coming home for your birthday?'

'No,' Freya said. 'I messed up my days off.'

'Any word on the man?'

'No. He's being very polite at work.'

'Well, that's good.'

'Not really.' Freya sighed. 'And I'd be mad to base staying on here just for a chance with him.' She was thinking out loud, really. 'He told me never to rely on him...'

Only that had been right at the start.

'And we were only together two months...'

'Freya,' Alison broke in. 'You're arguing with yourself.'

She had a lovely morning, spent mainly on the phone and opening the door to flower deliveries. There were some from her parents, from the staff at the Cromayr Bay birthing suite, and even a posy from Leah Roberts.

There was also a message in her inbox from

Malcolm, saying that if she was coming home for her birthday perhaps it would be good to catch up and see where it might lead…

Hell, no!

Freya slammed her computer shut.

And then later she felt the utter joy that came with the job of delivering a little one who'd share the same birthday as her.

Sophie Reece started to arrive in the world one foot first, causing her midwife more than a moment of internal panic. But there was Stella, coming in through the door and being amazing, followed by Dr Mina, who was the most calming presence. And soon there was the body out, with just the head to come.

'Patience…' Dr Mina said.

Guy Masters came in, and Richard did too, just in case this little one needed some more help. But, no, she was fine. Better than fine.

'Happy Birthday!' Freya said to the tiny new girl, once she was settled with her very delighted mum.

She was ready for her coffee break—seriously

so—as well as a sit-down, but that wasn't going to happen just yet.

'Happy Birthday!'

And there they all were. Stella, Kelly and Angela, and there was Rita, and Guy Masters, and even Richard, no doubt hauled back to come in while passing.

And there was a cake, with '30' written in glitter balls. Apparently Rita had made it.

But no candles.

'They set off the smoke detectors,' Stella explained.

Freya briefly met Richard's eye and tried, as she had that first day, to think of a quip about fire extinguishers.

But she didn't say anything—couldn't think of what to say that would fit the moment.

She read her card.

Best wishes
Richard Lewis

She looked up, about to ask him what the hell that was supposed to mean, but he was suddenly gone.

So she ate cake, and laughed with her friends,

and when Len came sniffing round for left-over cake for his animals Freya had it ready and wrapped for him.

It really was a lovely birthday.

Almost brilliant, in fact.

Just minus him.

But deep into her shift, coming up for nine o'clock, Freya was holding little Sophie while her mother got some very much deserved sleep and he came to the desk.

'Hello, *Richard Lewis*,' Freya snarked.

'Hello, Freya Ross,' he said, and took a seat at the computer.

'Why are you still here, Richard?' Stella checked. 'I thought you finished at six?'

'Yes, well, I'm covering for Simon, but I'm just about done.'

By the time little Sophie was asleep and about to be put in her crib he'd turned off the screen.

'I'm out of here.' But he spoke too soon, for immediately there came the ring of his phone.

'Excuse me,' he said to Stella as he answered the call.

But then he stopped being polite.

'What?'

He was *very* curt.

'I don't know—and I told you not to call me at work. I'm heading to a long case in Theatre, so I can't speak.'

He clicked off his phone.

'You are *such* a bastard.' Stella smiled. 'You just told me you were going home!'

'God, no,' Richard said. 'I'm checking into a hotel tonight. That was my mother. She's broken off her latest engagement and is currently staying with me and she's driving me crazy.'

Stella laughed and headed off.

Freya didn't know where to look, so she turned her eyes down to gaze at Sophie.

'Freya?' he said.

'What?'

She was still smarting about him writing *Best wishes* in her card and the use of his surname.

'You know how you used me?'

'I didn't *use* you, Richard, any more than you used me.'

'Yes, you did—but it doesn't matter right now.

I don't want to go to a hotel. Can you please use me again tonight?'

She laughed but did not answer him. And he watched as she walked away and put down the baby, taking time to wrap her carefully.

'This is the best birthday ever,' Freya whispered to little Sophie, and then she took a key from her pocket and headed back over to Richard.

'No strings,' he warned. 'And no talk of long-distance relationships and other such unmentionables.'

'Just sex, then?' Freya checked.

'Just that,' Richard agreed. 'But with my *very* best wishes.'

She slid over her key and he took it.

Richard hadn't really given much thought to his reaction when he entered her home. But it *was* a home now.

The scent of flowers hit Richard even before he had turned on the light, and when he did click it on the room felt different. There were deep red curtains that fell to the floor, and as he walked around he felt a soft rug underfoot. There were photos of family and friends on the shelves, and he knew he would love to be among them.

But they weren't friends.

They were lovers.

Only it felt a whole lot more than that.

And then he did something silly—which struck him as odd, because he never did things like that. He went to his car, where there was a mobile printer which he occasionally used for looking at cardiac tracings.

Today, though, he printed a photo of himself and tucked it behind one of the pictures on her shelf.

And then he headed to the kitchen. He saw there was still no coffee machine. But there were bananas on the bench and lots of lovely food in the fridge.

He went into the bathroom and saw there were new shelves there, and a shower curtain covered in pictures of shells that he recognised from her home in Cromayr Bay. When he turned on the taps the water ran hot within a minute, so Richard had a shower.

Then he put the door on the latch, so Freya could let herself in, and got into bed.

* * *

'Happy Birthday,' said Richard.

Freya sat on the bed. 'Everyone keeps asking me how it feels to be thirty.'

'How *does* it feel?'

'I delivered a baby for an eighteen-year-old today,' she said, and he smiled. 'I don't think I like it,' she admitted.

'You got a lot of flowers.'

'I did—and there are presents waiting for me at home.' Then she remembered the message from her ex and gave a little shake of her head.

'What?'

'Nothing,' Freya said, but then decided that if there was anyone she could tell it was Richard. 'My ex wanted to see if we might catch up.'

'And will you?' Richard asked. He found that he had to concentrate on keeping his voice even as a little snake of jealousy slithered up his chest.

'Of course not!' Freya laughed at the very thought.

And the little snake slithered away as she put her hands around his neck.

He was curious. 'Why did you break up?'

She gave a shrug. 'Just… Why does anyone break up? Why do *you* break things off with women?'

'Because I get bored.'

She looked into those hazel eyes that never seemed restless when they looked into hers.

'So why?' he persisted.

'We wanted different things,' Freya attempted. Only that wasn't right, because she did want a family one day. 'When I moved into my cottage he seemed to think it was his. And then, when I had the worst day at work ever—possibly the worst day of my life—I came home and told him.'

'And…?'

'He told me he was sorry, and he told me that he believed me when I said I'd done nothing wrong…'

'And…?'

'And then he went to work.'

There was silence as they stared at each other.

He would never have left her that day. Richard knew that.

And so too did Freya, because on the day when a woman he had never met had happened to be bleeding, he had dropped everything, swapped shifts, got in the car and driven her to Scotland.

'Freya,' Richard said, trying to give the other guy a chance. 'You sometimes have to ask for help. You can shut the world out with one glare, and...'

He could see behind the guarded look in her eyes though. Freya didn't need to stand semaphoring her needs—he read them and he felt them. Pity the fool who left her on a dark, dark day.

And more fool *him* if he didn't follow his heart, Richard thought as Freya stood up, peeled off her top and then unclipped her bra.

She slid down her jeans, and then her knickers too, and then climbed onto the bed, sat on his thighs and began to play with him.

'Shouldn't I be taking care of *you* on your birthday?' he asked as he reached up to trace the curve of her breast.

'I'm using you—remember?'

'So you are...'

And she was—but in the nicest of ways, imprinting his beauty on her mind. His flat nipples and the swirl of his chest hair. His dark hair and the soft skin of his balls as she held them. The way he grew to her touch, and the way he put his hand over hers and showed her just how rough he wanted her to be.

'Get on,' he said.

And as she did so she closed her eyes—not just because of the bliss, but because of the threat of tears, for she had thought they would never be together again.

Then she opened them and they stared at each other as he moved her hips, and then they melded into a kiss. He cupped her buttocks, feeling the softness of them, and feeling the way her hair was so silky as it spilled onto his cheeks.

He loved it that she held on to her cries. That this private woman, even as she squeezed her thighs and gripped him tight, even as she groaned and he felt her tension, did not reveal her hurt.

He held her by the shoulders and pushed her up, so he could see the concentration in her face and the parting of her lips as she came. He lifted and drove into her, and shot deep and she took every precious drop.

He loved it that they did not speak of love.

Not yet.

And that there was no need for either of them to ask if there had been anyone else since the last time.

Freya collapsed onto him.

'Happy Birthday,' he breathed again.

'It is.'

Truly it was.

But then, every day was made better, even the sad ones, when it was shared with him.

CHAPTER FOURTEEN

HE LOOKED TIRED, Freya thought when she woke the next morning. Even asleep he looked tired.

And it wasn't down to last night—she knew that.

He'd looked tired on the day she had met him and every day in between.

And if ever there was a man who deserved breakfast in bed it was him…

Richard woke to the sight of Freya holding a tray.

There was toast and *loads* of mushrooms, and a poached egg too, as well as a glass of orange juice. There was even a flower on the tray from one of her many birthday bouquets.

'What's this for?'

'I don't know.' Freya smiled. 'It's a rarity.'

'Well, thank you,' he said as she climbed into bed. 'What are you up to today?'

'Not much,' Freya said. 'On Friday I'm doing the London Eye at sunset with Stella, Kelly and Pat. I told them I wanted to cram in more of London before I went home and so we're going for my birthday.'

She looked over to him and they stared at each other. It was such a relief to be honest now about her leaving London.

'You're making friends, then?'

She nodded, but nothing had really changed—home was still home. So she addressed it. 'Richard, you warned me never to rely on you…'

'I know I did,' he said.

'So I'm making the best decision for *me*. I don't know yet if I'll go back to the birthing unit, I'm actually considering the main hospital. I've got a lot more experience now. I can go up a level—maybe two.'

The lack of rental income from her cottage was starting to bite, plus there was her rent in London…

'I'm not moving to Siberia.'

'I know.'

'Have you made up your mind about the private job?'

But they were teetering on the edge of long-distance relationship speak now, and he could not stand the thought of that. So instead of answering he gave her a kiss.

'I'm going to go.'

'Why?'

'Because I don't want to say something I might regret.'

He sounded as if he was cross with her, but it went a whole lot deeper than that. He didn't want to tell Freya that he too was considering moving.

To Cromayr Bay.

He would only say it when he was sure.

Until he'd properly thought it through, Richard wouldn't be sharing it with a soul.

It didn't stop his mother from finding out about it, though…

'What the *hell*, Richard?' Amanda said by way of welcome as he stepped through the door.

She was holding a letter.

'Did you open my mail?' Richard snarled.

'I was looking for an envelope and it just fell on the floor. Where the hell is Cromayr Bay and why on earth is the hospital there inviting you to come and have a look around?'

'It's none of your business.'

'Well, I'm making it my business. You would die of boredom. I know you, Richard. You're like me.'

'Don't terrify me, I beg you.'

'I mean it. You would seriously keel over from a lack of adrenaline. I should know. Have you *any* idea what it was like being married to your father and playing second bloody fiddle to his patients while looking at sheep all the time?'

Richard rolled his eyes.

'You've got an opportunity to go into the private sector.'

'I don't want to.'

'Oh, for God's sake stop lying to yourself.' Amanda was so appalled that she forgot to lie about her snooping. 'You've already signed the contract for the private hospital. You can't back out now.'

'You've seen that too?' Richard said, and he was so furious at this invasion of his privacy that he lashed out. 'I believe *you* signed a contract too…

"till death us do part"…and then you went and did it another two times.'

'Don't!' Amanda roared. 'I only married in church once and I meant every word.'

'Please…'

'Richard, for our twentieth wedding anniversary I told your father to get a locum, and he did, but then some patient needed him…'

'Mrs Lockley was terminally ill,' Richard reminded her wearily, because he knew the story well.

'And so was our marriage! Yet she survived longer than *we* did! Two more months, in fact. Your *hero* father didn't want to leave her, and in staying with her he neglected me. On the night of our wedding anniversary. When a locum could surely have dealt with things for once. But instead *he* had to be the one to go out to her.'

Richard just stood there, stunned, as his mother spun the mirror and for the first time ever he could see her side.

'Do you know,' Amanda raged, 'when he got back that night he asked me to make him some

Horlicks and then complained that there were lumps in it? I told him he wanted a live-in nurse or a housekeeper—not a wife. I gave him an ultimatum…'

And then she started to cry.

Really cry.

Not the dramatic tears he had grown up with.

'I thought he'd change when I threatened to leave him, that he'd beg me to stay, but instead he let me go…'

She really hadn't meant to end it. Richard knew that now.

'And then what did he go and do?' Amanda sobbed. 'He married our *housekeeper*. I'm sure there was something going on before…'

'No,' Richard said. Of that he was sure. 'He was gutted after you'd gone. He just moped around. He's a stubborn old mule, he would never have begged you to come back, and I guess Vera felt like routine.'

'You're positive there was nothing going on between them while we were still married?'

'I'm as certain as I can be,' Richard countered,

for though he'd always felt sure, he wasn't in the game of giving absolute guarantees. 'Anyway, they're divorced now, and I don't think it was a love match—though I bet she got all the lumps out of his Horlicks,' he said, and through her tears his mother laughed.

'I loved your father, Richard, very, *very* much. But he completely refused to compromise.'

'I can see that now.'

And now Richard wasn't only terrified of being like his mother, but like his father too. While he knew he'd shut Freya out, he wasn't merely being stubborn.

For this decision had to be his.

He had to be certain before he made it.

He would not offer her a life spent with even a shade of resentment. He'd grown up on that. So many ruined dinners because his father had been working.

He thought of Freya coming in with the breakfast tray, all smiling and being nice. Of course she'd understood that he'd had to dash off.

But what if it happened every morning?

Most nights?

'I don't think I was cut out to be a doctor's wife,' said his mother.

'I don't know about that,' Richard said. 'I don't think he knew what he had.'

Until it was gone.

Freya would soon be gone too.

But Richard would only make the move if he was absolutely sure he'd never begrudge the fact that he had.

He made his mother a cup of tea, and by the time he had done so Amanda had calmed down.

'Think again about going private, Richard. You wouldn't have signed the contract if it wasn't something you wanted.'

'I was just trying the idea on for size. It's signed—but it's not sealed, nor is it delivered.'

'What on earth are you doing, looking at Cromayr Bay?'

'I've met someone.'

'Freya,' his mother said.

'How do you know?'

'I spoke to her,' Amanda reminded him.

Richard remembered the first morning he

had awoken with Freya in his bed, when he had handed her the phone.

'She's Scottish,' Amanda added. 'So I'm guessing it's no coincidence.'

'Freya was born there—she's got family and friends there. She's tied to the place in a way that I'm not tied anywhere. I don't get your argument,' he went on. 'You're saying my father put too much into his work and never gave you enough attention. This move might be my way to negate all that.'

'It was never about the hours he worked, Richard. It was about the way he spent the hours he had at home. He gave all he had to his patients and left nothing for me.'

Richard had, up to this point, been quietly on the side of his father. He'd tried to stay loyal to both parents—of course he had—but in truth he had thought his mother a little shallow.

He didn't feel that now.

'I'm sorry,' Richard said.

'For what?'

'All the eye-rolls over the years.'

She smiled.

'But you are *never* going through my mail again.'

'I won't—but don't rush into this, Richard,' she warned. 'Don't end up like me…resenting the person you love.'

CHAPTER FIFTEEN

'RICHARD'S LEAVING.'

It was said just like that—and not even specifically to Freya.

They were lining up to board the London Eye, Stella, Kelly and Pat, all present, and Freya's heart felt as if it had fallen through a trap door.

'How's Von taking it?' Kelly asked.

'She's hoping to get off with him again at his leaving do!' Stella laughed, and then grimaced. 'Sorry, Freya. You had a bit of a thing going on with him for a while, didn't you?'

Freya nodded, and then pushed out a smile. 'I can't say I wasn't warned.'

The view from the London Eye was incredible.

It was the beginning of December and the sky was white, the trees bare and silver in the evening sun. Freya's heart twisted at the sight of the majestic city. Buckingham Palace, the Houses of Parliament, and the grey of the River Thames.

It was beautiful, and in that moment, high above London, Freya wished they might never have to come down.

Afterwards they went for a curry.

Freya's diary was filling up now, because it was nearing Christmas and she'd been invited to a couple of parties.

He would be gone by then.

She let herself into her flat and it was a relief to close the door and be home.

Home.

Freya looked at the curtains. Though they didn't block out the noise from the street she found the sound of cars and buses quite soothing now. And then she looked at the cushions, and the flowers sitting on the coffee table, and thought, yes, this was starting to feel like home.

Yet soon there would be no Richard.

No chance of seeing him at work…no hope of him asking to be 'used'.

And no scold in his voice when he told her off for her empty cupboards.

Oh, why did he have to leave *now*? Just when her world was coming right?

She went over to the shelf and looked at a photo of her little house in Cromayr Bay. Then she picked up the picture of her and her friends taken when they'd passed their midwifery exams.

And then she saw it.

Freya wasn't really one for efficient dusting, and she'd never taken the photos down until now.

But there it was.

A black and white picture of *him*, cut out on paper. And she wished, how she wished it was colour—because one day soon she might not remember the details of his eyes. Or the way he said her name—the change in his voice—so subtle at times that no one else would notice—that made her his lover and was audible only to her.

This is what you've lost, Freya.

And then her phone rang and the world suddenly felt better.

'Hello, Aunty Freya.'

Freya could hear the rise of elation in her friend's voice. 'Alison?'

'It's a girl—a little girl—four weeks early, but

everything's fine. She's not even an hour old yet...'

There was a waver in her voice and Freya closed her eyes as elation dimmed and Alison dipped into the valley of pain.

'She looks like her brother.'

And then, for the first time since that awful day, Freya knew what to say. If his sister looked like Andrew then it was certainly true. 'She must be perfect, then.'

For Andrew *had* been. Utterly, utterly perfect. From his soft brown hair down to his tiny toes.

And Freya had been so busy taking care of her friend, helping her through, that she'd somehow stuffed down her own grief.

It had been such a gut-wrenching loss. For Alison and Callum and their families, and for their friends and all who loved them too.

It was sometimes said that it took a village to raise a child.

Well, Cromayr Bay had mourned when Alison and Callum had lost theirs. He had been one of their own.

'When can you come and see her?'

'I'll see what I can do,' Freya said. 'I have to go in tomorrow, but I'll see if I can swap over the next couple of days. I'll call you in the morning. Go and enjoy…?'

'Eleanor,' Alison said.

It was hard to cry herself to sleep after such wonderful news, and Callum had been sending over pictures and, yes, Eleanor was utterly, utterly perfect.

But just after midnight Freya lay back on her pillow and sobbed.

Morning arrived and she woke with Richard's picture in the bed beside her. Before she headed for work she took a photo of it with her phone.

At work, she made a beeline for Stella.

'I hate to do this,' Freya said, 'but my friend just had her baby and Kelly has said that she'll swap with me. I'll work the weekend.'

'You haven't carried the Obstetric Squad pager yet, though,' Stella said, and then looked through the roster. 'It's okay—Pat's on, so she can do it. You need two more times observing and then Dr Mina needs to supervise you heading one.'

Freya nodded.

'What did she have?'

'A little girl—Eleanor.'

'Gorgeous,' Stella said.

Richard was coming out of ICU when Freya saw him. He was with Dominic.

'Hi.' Freya smiled.

'Freya,' he said as he passed. But a few steps on he excused himself and caught up with her. 'Are you free tomorrow?'

'I haven't got the energy to be used,' Freya admitted—because really she was terrible at flings.

When he was present she could forget for a while the hurt that awaited when he left. But when they were apart it was hell.

'I just wondered if you'd like to go to dinner.'

So you can tell me you're leaving?

She guessed it was for that.

A bastard he might be, to some, but she *liked* him—very much indeed—and perhaps he considered a hospital corridor with his registrar waiting not the ideal place for a goodbye.

'I can't,' Freya said. 'I'm away home after my

shift. I'm getting the overnight train. Alison had her baby late last night.'

'You'll be wrecked. What time does your train get in?'

'Seven—though I'll hang around at Waverley for the shops to open and then I am buying up pink.'

'So a little girl?'

'Eleanor.' Freya nodded. 'Then later we'll all be over to the Tavern to wet the baby's head.'

'Well…enjoy.'

Of course there were no offers from Richard to drive her this time, and she had an awful feeling this might be the last time she would see him.

He gave her a nice smile and then, because he was Richard, no conversation lasted very long without the interruption of his phone or pager.

This time it was the phone. 'My mother,' he said and pocketed it. 'I'll call her back in a moment.'

'How is she?'

'Well, she's found an apartment that isn't mine, so that's good. I don't know,' he said. 'I think that I misjudged her…'

And he left it at that.

Yet she desperately wanted to know more.

There was just so much to talk about—so much of each other to explore and to know.

And she had blown it, Freya knew.

CHAPTER SIXTEEN

WHEN SHE GOT to Waverley Freya drank coffee and ate almond croissants until the shops opened, and then went on a little frenzy of buying pink.

Then she took the train to Cromayr Bay. And as she crossed the bridge she gazed out over her home.

Home?

Yet London was also home.

Freya had never felt more confused in her life.

Visiting Alison was brilliant—to see her holding the tiny bundle and to know that they were both healthy and thriving, even though she might be struggling more than most new mothers today, was wonderful.

Callum went for a walk, and to meet some aunties who were arriving, and Freya had her first hold.

Oh, the baby was so soft and pink, and she had

beautiful little eyes and a pretty snub nose. And when Freya put her finger to Eleanor's hand little fingers closed around it.

'She's gorgeous—and she really does look like…' Freya hesitated and then made herself say his name. 'Andrew.'

Oh, grief was so hard when it was personal. At work she could do it, but here, sitting on the bed, it wasn't just Alison she was scared of hurting.

It was herself.

Richard, damn him, had been right again. *She* was grieving too. Because right about now she should be taking Andrew down to the café to give Alison and Callum a break.

And as she gazed down at Eleanor a tear splashed down Freya's cheek for a little toddler who wasn't there.

'Freya?' Alison asked. 'Talk to me.'

'I don't want to say anything that might upset you,' Freya admitted, and as she looked up she could see that Alison was crying too.

'You might,' Alison said, 'because I'm easily upset. Right now I'm both the happiest and the saddest I've ever been. Andrew should be here.'

'Yes,' Freya said, and her tears fell freely now. 'He should be.' And then she said something else too. 'I'm sorry if I haven't been here for you, Alison.'

'You have been.'

Alison was honest. She had no reason not to be.

'You were there every step when he was born, and at the funeral too. And you were here when I had the bleed and you're here now. Freya, losing Andrew changed things. Not for better or worse, but his death changed things. The world felt out of order. In many ways it still does. But even if you'd still lived down the street it was still something that I had to get through alone.'

'You've got Callum.'

'Of course I do. And we've got through this together. But there are parts of this that you can only do on your own. Look...'

She gestured to the window and Freya looked out, and sure enough there was Callum, walking on the green. And as Freya watched he ran the back of his hand over his eyes before heading back in.

He was crying alone and trying to be strong.

'Is there anything I can do?' Freya asked, not really expecting there to be. After all, if there was she'd have done it already.

If love could have fixed this, then there would have been a big brother in the room.

'Could you take this to him for me?' Alison asked, and untied a little pink balloon from Eleanor's crib. 'Can you tell him he has a sister? And can you buy a blue one for him?'

'Of course.'

And they were friends again—well, they always had been, but they had both needed to find their own way to grieve.

The door opened and in came Callum, all smiles but with glassy eyes, and several aunts and uncles who had just arrived.

'Freya!' His voice was bright. 'We've waited for you to get here but we can wait no more. We're wetting the bairn's head over at the Tavern tonight.'

'I can't wait.' Freya smiled.

She headed down to the gift shop with the pink balloon in hand, and bought a blue one as Alison had asked. She bought flowers and a little wind-mill too.

Freya hadn't been to the cemetery since Andrew's funeral, yet she found his grave easily, for that sombre walk was etched in her heart.

She had been looking out for Alison then, worried that after surgery and all the exhausting emotion her friend might faint.

Alison almost had.

Freya walked down the path and there it was, his tiny grave. She looked at his name and the dates on the little cross. Two days he had lived, but he would never be forgotten.

'You have a wee sister,' Freya said, though the wind took her words, and it was so cold the heat of her tears stung her cheeks as she tied the balloons and then put the little windmill into one of the pots and watched it whirling for a while.

The wind was biting as she walked the short distance to her home, and once there Freya lay on the bed, a jumble of emotions pounding through her heart.

Was she considering staying in London for a

chance with a man who had told her never to rely on him?

Only it wasn't just for Richard—she was coming to love the place too. The noise and the people and the flower seller who had, for no reason, given her a rose the other day. And grumpy old Len. Oh, and not forgetting cynical Stella.

Yet she loved it here too.

At six, Freya dressed for the celebrations.

She did her hair and her make-up, and put on a dark red wool dress, black stockings and boots.

She made every effort—because she was thrilled and happy and she wanted to celebrate Eleanor's arrival. And she was so pleased that they'd waited until she was there.

And then she put on a warm overcoat and headed for the Tavern.

The party was in full swing when she arrived, and Freya knew she had been wrong before. The hardest thing wasn't walking into a pub knowing your ex might be there.

It was knowing he couldn't possibly be.

She hung her coat up and then headed over to the bar, where a large whisky was thrust into her

hand. It was as if the entire town was out, cele-
brating the marvellous news.

Betty and Dr Campbell were in good spirits and
even Leah Roberts had found a babysitter and was
there with her husband, Davey.

It was absolutely the best night.

Even with a piece of her heart missing.

A big piece.

Actually, now she thought about it, just a tiny
part of her heart remained.

And then she saw him.

He was standing in the doorway, wearing a suit
and looking around…

Not Malcolm.

Richard.

She thought she must be seeing things, surely,
but then she met his eyes and gave him an uncer-
tain smile as he walked over.

'What are you doing here?' Freya asked.

'I've got a booking in the restaurant,' Richard
said. 'If you'd care to join me?'

The newly refurbished Tavern Restaurant was
both stunning and familiar. The gorgeous tradi-
tional Scottish stone walls had been retained, but

a deep moss-green carpet gave the momentary feeling that they were outside a rugged castle. The tables were dressed simply in white, and in the candlelight the silverware gleamed, while on each tablecloth stood a small vase holding thistles.

And she was here with Richard.

Over and over Freya had to keep telling herself that—not that she could forget it—in order to hold on to the dream, else he might disappear.

They ordered drinks and made small talk with Gordon and between themselves as they waited for them to arrive. But when Gordon started to go through the menu, she blinked at the slightly impatient note to Richard's voice.

'Could we have a moment, please?'

'Certainly…' Gordon nodded.

Freya looked over to Richard and could see his discomfort. And then she knew why he was here. They had been more than a fling—they both knew that—and now, Freya guessed, knowing she was in Scotland, Richard had decided that she deserved a little more than a hospital corridor goodbye.

'I'm not sure if you've heard,' Richard said, 'but I've given in my notice.'

'I heard.' Freya nodded and thought her voice was a little high, as if braced for pain.

'I've been doing a lot of thinking,' Richard said. 'I didn't want to rush into things. I don't like snap decisions.'

'But they're what you do best,' Freya pointed out. 'You think on the run.'

'At work, perhaps,' Richard agreed, 'but I've had fifteen years of training and supervision and amazing mentors. When it comes to matters of the heart I have no clue. I didn't exactly have exemplary role models in that department...' Then he paused, because that wasn't quite right. 'I never thought I'd be asking my mother for relationship advice, but I have been.'

'And what advice did she give?'

'To take the private hospital position and to hell with you—and, frankly, I agreed with her.'

And then he saw Freya's pain, and knew that his job, when at all possible, was to take away pain.

He took her hand. 'I agreed with her for about two weeks,' he said. 'I accepted the role with Marcus and gave notice at the Primary. But then I spoke to my father too.'

'And…?'

'I didn't ask him for advice,' Richard said. 'Instead I gave it. I told him that he could quit telling me he was lonely, because it was his own bloody fault. He lost the love of his life. I don't intend to do that.'

Freya looked up.

'My ties to London are through work and friends. I didn't go to school there. I don't have family there. I understand that this is your home—the place you love. Now, I'm not sure if Cromayr Bay Hospital is big enough for me, but I'll try it for size if it means being with you. I love you.'

She had it all in that moment.

The gift of his love was like a shiny parcel, momentarily blinding her, and this gift came with a velvet box. He opened it and there was a ring. She could see it, but not really see it, for it was blurred by the tears in her eyes.

They were not all happy tears.

She had everything she wanted, Freya thought. Yet all she truly wanted was him. Richard.

'That won't be necessary.' She looked up and saw his face bleach pale, realised he thought she was rejecting the ring. 'I mean the move—not the ring.'

'Freya…?'

'I went on the London Eye and it was an amazing view,' Freya said. 'Not better, nor more beautiful than here, just different. Richard…'

She tried to explain the jumble of her feelings with a heart that was pounding and a head that was slightly giddy.

'After we broke up I was scared that I was thinking of extending my contract in London just in the hope of getting back with you…'

There—she had said it.

'I'd been warned by several people—including yourself—not to count on a future with you. And so I made my decision based on what I knew. I'm falling in love with London and, as exhausting as it is, I love the work. And…' She could be honest now. 'I love *you*. I had to give us a chance.'

'You're staying in London?'

Freya nodded. 'Can you retrieve your notice?'

'God, yes,' Richard said.

He slipped the ring on her slender finger and they toasted their news with a single malt whisky that tasted amazing on his lips when they kissed.

'And now,' Richard said, 'I'm having that game pie.'

He'd been waiting for it for a very long time.

CHAPTER SEVENTEEN

A WEDDING IN Cromayr Bay would never pass unnoticed. That was the beauty of home, Freya thought as she dozed on the train on her way up to Waverley.

In the end it was the bride who had struggled to get time off from work. She'd had one more Obstetrics Squad Emergency to attend before she could be signed off, and Stella had wanted it done before she renewed her contract. As well as that, her trips to Scotland had meant she had very limited days off to indulge in planning a wedding.

A winter wedding.

Richard, though, didn't start his new contract until the end of February, so he had been up to Cromayr Bay a few times without Freya, and had finally sorted out his phone so that Freya could call him.

It was a silent coach, so instead of calling she

texted him to say she'd arrived at Waverley and was taking the train to Cromayr Bay. She was secretly hoping that he would meet her.

I'll see you in the morning, then.

Freya was dying to see him, but there was just so much to fit in.

Has your mother arrived?

Not yet.

They were both worried about that, and pretending not to be. Richard's parents hadn't been in the same room without a judge present for seventeen years. But he refused to think of that now.

Richard loved Cromayr Bay. It had the bracing, salty, sharp air that his body required. It was a place he could retreat to and a place he could learn to relax in, for that was necessary indeed.

And then his parents arrived.

The day before the wedding.

The concierge at the Tavern, who doubled as

the duty manager, called Richard down to meet Amanda, who stood in Reception bristling.

'My room's not ready.'

'It will be soon,' Richard said.

'You don't understand,' she hissed. 'Your *father's* here. He's over there at the bar.'

Great.

A fight between his parents on the eve of his wedding was the last thing he needed, and so after a few nips of whisky with Freya's brothers, along with many other new friends who had joined them, the bear retired to his cave.

And then a horrible thing happened.

From the room above his own he heard his mother laugh.

Not a bad thing on its own.

But then he heard the unmistakable rumbling sound of his father's laugh too…

By morning Richard had decided that, while the restaurant might have been refurbished, the squeaking beds at the Tavern still needed an overhaul.

He *had* to tell Freya—except it wasn't Freya who answered her phone. Instead it was Alison.

'No, you *can't* speak to her!'

Freya frowned when she heard Alison's firm tone.

She had seen that it was Richard calling, but, given that she was getting her make-up done, Alison had taken the call.

'Let me speak to him,' Freya said, holding out her hand for the phone.

'No!'

It would seem that Alison was taking her Matron of Honour duties very seriously.

'Is it a medical emergency?' she asked Richard.

It would seem not.

'Are you going to jilt the bride?'

Freya rolled her eyes and snapped her fingers, indicating that she wanted to be given the phone, but Alison had other ideas.

'Then there's nothing that can't wait. Anything urgent, have the best man call *me*—not the bride!'

The flowers in Freya's bouquet were the very same as the ones she had bought on the day she had decided to give London a go. The bunch of pale lilacs perhaps didn't appear a very opulent display, but they were now the flowers that made her 'cheer up, love'.

And Freya was both cheered up and nervous as she felt her father's arm beneath her hand and she walked towards the love of her life.

Richard did not stare ahead, instead he turned and watched her every step.

Yes, Officer, I will remember what she was wearing for ever.

Her dress was the colour of a pearl moon as it hung over the local bridges, and on her feet were silk ballet pumps. The flowers he couldn't name, but he knew that she bought them often.

As for her hair… Freya wore it down, and yet it sprang up in curls about her face. Wild and dark, it moved with her.

Make-up? That he would never recall. For as her father let go of her arm and Richard took her hands nothing else mattered.

'You made it,' he said.

'Just.'

They shared a smile and a couple of words in that moment before proceedings commenced.

The vicar spoke of the seriousness of the vows

before them as he addressed the packed congregation. And Richard's voice was lovely and clear as he repeated the words which became his promise to her.

'To love and to cherish, till death do us part.'

Those words had always made her a little sad, talking of death at a wedding. And yet they were actually rather gorgeous to hear, she thought, when she was being held by Richard's eyes.

He was taking this as seriously as she, Freya knew. He had avoided and hidden from love, but—like heartache—love found you and chased you until you either denied it or faced it.

And they faced each other now, and smiled as they were pronounced man and wife.

Richard kissed his bride. Their smiling lips met, but he felt the tremble of hers beneath his as emotion caught up with her.

'It's okay,' he said, and briefly held her, 'we've got each other for life.'

They turned and walked down the aisle to see many smiling, friendly faces. Some were familiar to Freya but new to Richard, and some were the other way around.

Freya knew there were friends from the Primary, who had made the trip, but first she smiled to her parents and her brothers, and then to Richard's parents, who stood side by side.

Freya seriously hoped there would be no arguing between them tonight—though Richard had told her it was his parents' problem if they did.

And then there was Kelly, Stella, Pat, Rita and Angela and, it seemed, half the anaesthetics department, including Dominic, who was looking forward to having his old boss back.

They stood and smiled for the camera, and it actually wasn't too painful because Freya had insisted on only a few formal shots.

'It's too cold to stand outside,' she had said, and so, surprisingly quickly, they were back at the Tavern, in the gorgeous new function room at the very top of the hotel.

Freya hadn't seen it before. Only Richard, who had organised things, had been inside.

It was stunning.

Huge long tables were dressed with tall white candles, and there were large bunches of wild Scottish flowers.

It felt as if they were in a castle, Freya thought. And the arched windows looked out on the view she loved—though she really didn't notice the view as Richard made his speech.

He kept it short and sincerely thanked everyone, especially those who had travelled from afar—'Including me,' he quipped.

He got through the formalities, then admitted a truth.

'I never thought I'd be doing this,' Richard said, 'but I am so honoured to be here. As some of you will know, Freya and I have two places we call home—one in London, another here in Cromayr Bay. I love them both. And, as I've found out, so too does my *wife.*'

He paused, not for effect, but more because it didn't even sound odd to be saying that. It felt right.

And it sounded just right to Freya, too, and she gave him a smile before he spoke on.

'It's not the house, or the location, or even the view. It's the *people* who make a place feel like home. But at the end of the day you close the door.

Freya,' he said, 'I will always be happy to come home to you.'

It was the loveliest day of her life.

Freya found out via the best man about a few of Richard's more colourful escapades, and she shared a smile with Stella. She couldn't say that she hadn't been warned.

And then there was a toast to the bridesmaids and the formalities were done.

Almost.

'This is our first dance,' Richard said.

'As man and wife?'

'No,' Richard said. 'This is our very first dance.'

Indeed it was, Freya realised.

She and Richard hadn't yet made it to the cinema, let alone the dance floor. And so it was utter bliss to rest in his arms for a moment and savour their first dance. One she would remember for ever.

Perhaps they should be gazing into each other's eyes, Freya thought, but it was nice just to be held and to breathe in the scent of him and enjoy a quiet moment.

That was how he made her feel. Safe in his

arms, whatever the adventure. And he made her feel something else too…

She looked up to him. 'I want to break out of my skin and dance,' Freya admitted, and they both knew how rare this was, since she was not a dancing type of person.

'When we're alone,' Richard said in his most deadpan, sexiest voice, 'you can certainly break out of your skin and dance. I might even join you!'

He made her toes curl.

And he made her smile in a way no one else did.

But then she saw something.

His parents were dancing and it didn't look strained.

In fact, they were gazing into each other's eyes.

'Richard…' She raised her head, but he knew what she had seen.

'I know.' He spoke low into the shell of her ear. 'That's why I tried to call you. I think they might be getting back together.'

'No!'

'Yes,' he said, and then he lifted her chin, so that she looked deep into his eyes. 'We'll never be like them. I'm going to take care of the love we've found.'

'And me,' Freya told him.

They would both take the best of care of this very precious love.

EPILOGUE

'BUT WHY WOULDN'T you have him *here*?' Amanda asked.

They were discussing Richard and Freya's baby, which was due in three weeks.

'Firstly, it might be a she,' Richard pointed out to his mother. 'Secondly, it should be Freya's choice. We're going up at the weekend for a few days and we'll decide then.'

Except that they wouldn't.

Richard didn't know it yet, but Freya was already in labour.

She did *not* want a false alarm, nor to get to the hospital and find out that she wasn't very far along and so she had been keeping quiet.

But she was certain now.

The contractions were fifteen minutes apart and they were getting stronger. The decision as to where to have their baby had now, as of this afternoon, become a moot point.

They went home to Cromayr Bay a lot.

Richard's job remained as constant and as high pressure as ever, but now, instead of him flying away, they drove to there. And if they didn't feel like driving they took the train, because it really was the most wonderful train journey and so relaxing.

Apart from at Newcastle. Each time the train pulled into there Freya and Richard would exchange a glance as they recalled that text exchange that had nearly put an end to them for ever.

Her cottage was slowly coming on, and Richard loved their time there so much that a role at Cromayr Bay Hospital still wasn't completely off the cards.

After a couple of days spent catching up with friends and loved ones, or simply unwinding alone together, they'd get back in the car, or board another train, and come home.

Freya had fallen in love with London.

Properly.

She had started to fall in love with it when she

and Richard had broken up. It had been her friends there who had helped her through, even if they hadn't known just how broken-hearted she'd really been.

They had both been a bit undecided as to where they wanted the baby to born.

Amanda, though, had clearly made up her mind. 'I hope you have it here.'

'Why?' Richard asked. 'I thought you enjoyed your stay at the Tavern.'

'I did.'

'Good.'

There had been no reference to that night—no mention, no comment. If Richard hadn't been unlucky enough to land the room beneath them he might never have known.

'Richard,' Amanda said now, 'can I have a word?'

'Go ahead.' He would not be following her into the kitchen so they could speak quietly. 'I'll be telling Freya what you say anyway, so you might just as well say it here.'

'Very well. Now, I know after I called things off with Roger, that I said I was through with men but… Richard, please don't roll your eyes. Your father and I have been seeing each other since your wedding.'

Richard said nothing.

'We haven't rushed into anything. We've both done that before, and we didn't want to put you through another wedding, but we…we got married last week.'

Richard just stood there.

'It was a quiet wedding,' Amanda said. 'We didn't want a fuss—or rather I didn't want a fuss—and so we went to Gretna Green, and had a little honeymoon at the Tavern.'

'Why aren't you both here to tell me?' Richard asked. 'Is he too busy working?'

'No, we were both going to come, but then we decided that it might be a bit much for the two of us to turn up at your door saying everything's all right now. While it is for us—well, we know that it can't have been easy on you. That's why I came alone.'

He smiled and kissed his mother the perpetual bride. 'Congratulations. And I really do mean that.'

Freya kissed her too, and then Richard got out some champagne. As he did so, Freya excused herself and went into the bedroom.

The pains were getting strong now, that was for certain, but also there was a need to be alone as she thought of Richard and all he had been through with his parents.

For what?

Nearly two decades apart and a whole lot of heartache in between—because neither would back down or consider the other person's side.

Freya knew she had a lot to be grateful for.

Of course, when she came out Amanda showed them the wedding pictures, and Freya made herself scarce now and then, because she wanted to tell Richard that she was in labour alone.

At last Amanda looked at the time. 'I really do have to go or I'll miss my train…'

'Does my father want his dinner?' Richard asked, and his voice was wry.

'No, he's taking me out.'

'Good for you.'

They saw her out, and although Richard hadn't

jumped up and down at the news, Freya could tell he was pleased.

'At least it will make things easier on the baby.' Richard commented once she had gone. 'Just plain old Grandma and Grandpa Lewis. We'll have to wait until he's old enough to fill him in on the last twenty years.'

He recalled what they had been discussing before his mother had shared her news. They *did* need to make their minds up.

'Freya, if you want to have the baby in Scotland then…'

'We're having it here, Richard.'

'You don't have to make your mind up now.'

'The baby already has. The contractions are ten minutes apart.'

'Is that why you kept ducking out of the room?'

'Yes.'

But she didn't duck out for the next one, and he felt her stomach turn to rock.

'They're getting worse,' Freya said.

'They're getting *stronger*,' Richard teased, because he heard a lot of midwife-speak every day at work.

But then he saw the chink of anxiety in those guarded green eyes that only he could read.

'Do you want to go to the hospital now?'

'Yes.'

It was a wise choice, Freya had decided. The Underground wasn't an option, and she knew the traffic was terrible on a Friday night, even though the Primary wasn't a particularly long drive from where they lived.

'Oh, God!' she shouted as they didn't even move an inch through one traffic-light-change.

'You're doing really well.'

'No, seriously, Richard! I can't have it in a car.'

'You're not going to. We'll be there soon.'

'How soon?'

'Soon-*ish*,' he said.

'I'm stuck in traffic with an anaesthetist and I'm going to be too far along for an epidural!'

Richard said nothing.

And then there was the hospital, and the ugly grey building had never looked more beautiful to Freya.

He held her hand as they walked the terribly long walk along the yellow line, and when they pushed open the doors to the maternity unit Freya had never been more relieved to be anywhere in her life.

'Freya—welcome!'

Stella had got her name right for once. But she was a patient now, Freya realised as she was helped into a gown and examined.

'You are doing an amazing job,' Stella told her. 'You're four...nearly five centimetres dilated.'

'Only four centimetres!'

'Nearly five—and that's a great time to call for an anaesthetist,' Stella said, because that was on Freya's birthing plan.

Richard said nothing, even though he'd guessed that Freya wasn't really about to have the baby. After all, he had given many, many epidurals.

He said nice things as he felt her disappointment that she wasn't further along. 'You're well into active labour. Sometimes having an epidural too early can slow down the contractions.'

And again he said nothing when Stella informed them that Dominic would be getting to them very soon—well, just as soon as he could...

Richard knew that if Dominic was delayed when his boss's wife was here then it would be with good reason.

Yet after some more waiting Richard better understood just how awful it was to see someone you loved in pain and be unable to help them. Worse, to be able to help them but to have to step back.

But then the door to D5 was opened and a very nice sight for any labouring mother was there.

'Hi!'

Dominic was a bit breathless, but his smile was so nice he put Freya at ease immediately. And both Freya and Richard knew and trusted everyone in this room.

'I think I'm in love with Dominic,' Freya said when the pain had eased.

'I bet you say that to all the anaesthetists,' Stella teased.

It was a gentle evening.

Dr Mina came in and checked that all was well, and as always she made Freya feel calm, and then Freya dozed on and off and later was thrilled when the night staff came on and she saw that her midwife was Kelly.

Things really had moved along because now, just after ten, when Kelly examined her she told her it was time to start to push.

The lights stayed dimmed and with Kelly's encouragement she was soon pushing effectively. It was a good epidural that had been administered, because she could feel the pressure of the contractions but not the pain—though it was still exhausting first-baby work.

And then the room started to fill up.

Pat came in to take the baby.

And Dr Mina came back in too.

Freya assumed it was just because she was a member of staff.

Not so.

The room was still calm, but Richard could see that forceps were fast becoming an option.

He pulled back Freya's leg as Pat did the same on the other side, while Dr Mina tied on a plastic gown.

'Freya,' Kelly urged, 'I want you to give me a big push *now*.'

The last moments were here, and Freya went inside herself.

'Freya,' Kelly said again, and it felt as if her voice came from afar. 'I need you to *push*.'

'Good girl,' Dr Mina encouraged her.

Except Freya was both scared and spent. She was slight and slender, and Richard wasn't, and this baby was large.

'Freya?'

She opened her eyes to him and Richard stared deep into the darkest of greens. He loved this sullen woman and the fight it had taken to gain her trust. He loved how she did not jump to anyone's command nor readily hand over her guarded heart.

Yet with time she had handed it to *him*.

And now he watched as she rallied again, and then, deep in the early hours of morning, a promise for the future arrived.

A boy.

He lay on Freya's stomach, curled up and stunned for half a moment, but then he let out a husky cry.

'Richard?' Pat said, and held out scissors for him to cut the cord.

Unexpectedly, he declined.

For once neither Richard's head, hands nor heart were steady.

The boy was perfect.

Freya pulled him up into her arms and held him, taking in every finger and toe and tasting his breath as he cried.

'Do we know his name?' Kelly smiled as she wrote on the little birth tags.

'William,' Freya said, and looked down at little William, unable to believe he was really here.

And then everyone melted away and they were left alone to have time to get to know their baby.

Richard had a hold of his son. He held him to his chest in those lovely strong arms.

Freya had never felt so happy and so balanced with the world.

'There are going to be a lot of people thrilled to know you're here,' he said to his son, in that lovely low voice.

And there were.

Yes, soon the phone calls would start, and visitors would be welcomed in, but for now it was phones off and time alone.

For both knew the importance of time.

Time together, spent as a family.

* * * * *

LET'S TALK

Romance

For exclusive extracts, competitions
and special offers, find us online:

 facebook.com/millsandboon

 @millsandboonuk

 @millsandboon

Or get in touch on 0844 844 1351*

For all the latest titles coming soon,
visit millsandboon.co.uk/nextmonth

*Calls cost 7p per minute plus your phone company's price per
minute access charge